CUPID

IS

STUPID

But you don't have to be.

By

Aaron Bryant Jr.

Copyright 2005 by Aaron Bryant Jr.

All rights reserved. Without limiting rights under copyright reserved above. No part of this book may be reproduced, stored in or introduced into a retrieval system, or transmitted, in any form, or by any means(electronic, Mechanical, photocopying, recording, or otherwise), with out prior written consent from the author, except brief quotes used in reviews.

The cover was done by Dixie Press.
The editing was done by Angela Hooper.

Dedications

Thank you Jehovah Jesus, my Lord and Savior, whose forgiveness I am in constant need of. I thank you Father, who can make all things possible for those who believe.

I dedicate this book to the memory of my father, Aaron S. Bryant Sr., who passed away on 7/12/93, at the age of 51. We all miss you still.
And to my mother, Alice Bryant, who is still alive, and I am glad she will see my first book.

I would also like to dedicate this book to my three girls, Shadavia, Jessica, and Shaquanna. You three are my inspiration. I love you all so much. I hope as young writers, you will follow your dreams, as I have followed mines.

I would like to thank my sibling, Susan, Sandy, Edward Shanice, Rayshawn, and Myshawn for their support. I would also like to thank my Transit family for their encouragement.

Special thanks go out to my Jersey people, Jackie, Kisha, and Chris. Thanks for reading my screenplay of Cupid is Stupid, and for your encouragement. You three were the first to read it, and enjoyed it so much, that it greatly encouraged me. Again I say, Thanks

CHAPTER ONE:
THE BOYS

"Damn, you look so good. Mmmmmm. Good enough to eat. What are you wearing? You smell so good. I was just messing with that other stuff. You know you are the only dish for me. You know you're important to me, so I'll do all the things you like. Of course I'll do that. You know I like the way you taste. How do you taste? You know. Stop playing. I might bite a little, because I know you'd like that. You look good today, but you look good every day. Good enough to eat. Of course I got a big tongue. Oh stop it; I'm not going to show it to you. OK. I'll give you just a peak. Oh you like the way it looks. Well I wanna taste you too. I can, when? Right now, OK. Umm yeah, you taste so good baby, so nice and juicy."

A large African and Indian looking man is sitting at the counter eating a hamburger. He is talking to it.

"Yeah, I like that too." stats Tonka. Tonka is eating his hamburger as if in a trance. His eyes are close, as he cherishes each chew. His spell is broken by a beautiful, light skin lady, who taps him on the shoulder. Her hair is done very stylish, and she is wearing a slick, black business suit. The suit makes her look professional, but she can not hide her sistah looking body, which drives the men around her wild. She did not work because she did not need to. She has doe, but likes the business look. Tonka almost jumps at her touch, which broke his romantic encounter.

"I'm sorry to disturb you, but I heard your conversation." Carmen states. She wants to use her sensual voice, but she is too busy enjoying her own arousal. She does not appear to be breathing heavily, but her chest is moving up and down like she is out of breath. The top part of her forehead is moist, but it is not the only thing wet. Carmen hands him her card. It is not her intention to approach a man because they usually approach her. She usually gives men a hard time, but this time she is caught of guard. Entice by words not meant for her. She is operating on cruise control because her instincts are all gone. Lost to this new sensation she is feeling. I guess it is not new, but she has not felt this way in such a long time, that it feels new to her.

"Call me." She says like a command, but it comes out like a plea. She stares into his eyes with passion, and then walks away. A man sitting at the table glances over to peek at Carmen's butt as she passes. He then jumps slightly, remembering who he is with, but it is too late. The stern look and twisted lips from his girlfriend shows that he will be spending a few nights on the couch.

Tonka puts the card in his pocket, but he never looks to see how beautiful Carmen is from behind. All he wants to do is to get back to his first love, his true love, his only love, which is his food. Tonka looks at his plate and sees it is empty. "Scandalous." He says to himself.

A few feet away, a middle aged waitress with grayish black hair, and a tired look on her face, watches Tonka. She is holding a plate with two hot dogs on it. She squeezes a smile out of her tired face because she can see how sad Tonka looks, when he sees his plate empty. She walks over and sits the plate before Tonka, and then she steps back to watch him. Another short waitress sees her looking at something, and looks to see what she is looking at. When she sees her watching Tonka, she stops what she is doing, to watch as well.

Tonka sees the two franks on a plate in front of him, and perks up immediately. "Ummmmmmm, Manajatwa."

The two waitresses burst out laughing. They try to cover their mouths realizing how loud they had laughed, but they can't control themselves. Their tired look is erase by laughing faces. Tonka should be able to hear them, but he is focusing on his food. Some customers see them laughing, but can't see what they are laughing at. The boss hears the choppy laugh of one waitress, and the slow steady laugh of the other. The boss approaches them, and knows immediately what they are laughing at.

"Go on you two, we have people to serve." The Boss scolds, as the two waitresses continue laughing, but get back to work. "This man paid for my children to get through college, and is going to pay for my boat, so you let him eat."

Later on that evening, Tonka is sitting in the same diner with three of his friends.

"That is how it happened right over there at the counter." Says Tonka.

"Yeah right." Jason states.

Jason is medium built, brown skin, African American. He is around five foot ten inches, and has the look of a play boy. He is wearing shiny jewelry, and Rolex watch. Stereotypes would place him as a drug dealer, but he makes an honest living. Growing up, Jason failed at most things he attempted. He tried to go to college, but was not focused enough. He tried a trade school, but was not focused enough. He even tried to sell drugs for a minute, when his mother put him out, but was not focused enough. Thank God that did not last long because his true friends, the ones at this very table, pulled him away from that. Daren, who saw Jason's magnetic personality, advised him to try selling things for a living. Jason now sells cars for a living, and is good at it. He was always the most popular person in school, and wants to be the center of attention at every party. Yeah you know the type. Most people would think that is a sign of security, and would say he is very bold; however, the few that know, and are smart enough to look beneath the surface, know it is a sign of insecurity. The loudness and flashy things work as lures for the sexiest of women. Having good looks doesn't hurt either. Jason has a main girl, Tammy, who he lives with. She is a good girl who works and treats him nice, but Jason messes around on her. I know what you are thinking, but it is not because she is a good girl. He would have fooled around on a bad girl too. In his mind it would be selfish to keep himself to one woman. In Jason's defense, Tammy knew what type of man he was when she met him. She was lured in by his jewelry and charm, even though she knew he had a girlfriend. It's strange how the things that attracted her to him, are now the things that haunts her when Jason is hanging out late.

"It's easy for him to pull women because he is so charming." She would think to herself. That was followed by hours of wondering why she puts up with him. Then she would have a pillow full of tears to soak herself to sleep on. Funny how she never thought about the woman she pulled Jason away from, and her tears. She only wondered was the next woman out there, preparing Jason to replace her.

Now she wished she had chosen better, but it was too late. She was in love. Others would argue love is not a reason, but she would spend half of her free time, justifying why she should stay with him. "He's so handsome, and he can be loving when he wants to." She would think to herself. Translation, he acts like he loves me when he wants some. "Oh he gives me money. He makes good money at his job." She would justify to her friends. Translation, he gives me money, but then borrows it back, and never pays it back. "He doesn't spend time with me, but the time we spend is quality time." She **would argue. Translation, he waxes that ass when we have sex.**

"You're trying to keep it Jigga like me." Jason states while looking at Tonka. Tonka is about to reply, but someone else cuts in.

A six feet, slightly overweight, African American male speaks. He has on average clothing, and his hair is faded on the sides. He is dark skin, and has no facial hair.

"Come on Jason. You know Tonka's style. The ladies like his long hair, which is the Cherokee Indian in him." States Daren. "How does she look Tonka?"

Daren is married with no children. He works as a Social worker for the City. It is a job he halfway likes, but hey, it pays the bills. Any job is a good job as long as it allows him to take care of his wife. That is what he would always say.

"She is cute." Tonka states as he looks up from his bowl of soup with the expression, "Hey I'm eating."

"Oh come on Tonka, we need more information than that." Dean states. Dean is a brown skinned man around six feet, and one inch. He has a bald head, but still has the side burns and a slight mustache. He is dressed in a shirt and a tie, and works as a Pharmacist in Manhattan. To hear Dean talk, he likes what he does, but there is something missing from his life. Like most people, he has not figured it out yet, but he commits to whatever he takes on. Dean calls it determination, but his friends call it stubbornness. All in all, Dean is a simple guy. He knows what he wants, and goes for it.

"So tell me Tonka, was her body banging?" Dean asks.

Tonka looks up from his second bowl of soup. "Look, I was not looking at her body. I though she was rude to interrupt my lunch. She gave me a card. Her name is Jennifer or something, and she was dressed nicely. Now can I eat in peace?"

Daren thinks for a second. "Hold up." Daren states, as everyone focuses on him. "What's her number?"

Tonka reaches in his pocket, and pulls out her card. "595-1110" Tonka shoots out.

"Oh no. Tonka is messing with Daren's sloppy seconds." Dean teases. As they all laugh.

"Yo, that is Jennifer's girl friend you were talking to. She looks nice, but she usually dates rich guys, not Train operators." Daren states.

"What do you mean Train operators like me? I got doe." Tonka shoots back. Tonka is only joking because he knows he makes more than Daren, so Daren is not trying to insult him.

"I'm not talking about that baby deer you had for lunch." Daren jokes back, but he is the only one laughing. He states, "Yawl don't get it, that was funny."

"We get it, a baby dear is a doe, but it was corny." Tonka replies.

Dean and Jason lean over towards each other, and are whispering. Daren prepares himself because he knows something stupid is coming out of one of their mouth.

"So Daren, what are you doing checking out your wife's friend, and how do you know her number?" Jason states and Dean laughs.

"Caller ID. You egg head." Daren shoots back. "You guys know I don't mess around." This is something Daren is proud of.

Tonka looks at Daren and holds out his fist for some dap. "Double up?"

"You know it." Daren states and gives Tonka a pound. "Friday is good for you?"

"Perfect." Tonka states, and then returns to his soup.

"I'll set it up." Daren confirms.

"Tonka can you help Dean. I have tried, but he's without hope." Jason states with a smile. Dean rolls his eyes.

"Look at him rolling his eyes like a little girl." Jason states.

"I don't need your type of help." Dean replies back.

Tonka looks at both of them. "What happened?"

"Dean is still on his love search. He wants to find romance, so I tried to hook him up with some ladies I knew." Jason states with a grin.

"Hoes and freaks. That is your idea of romance, not mines anymore." Dean defends himself.

"What? Something wrong with my hook ups?" Jason asks.

"Wrong is not the word, like that last one you set me up with." Dean complains as the other listen.

"What was wrong with the last one? She was cute, body banging, and ready. I knew I should have kept her for myself." Jason states.

"You guys act like they're baseball cards, ready to be traded." Daren states as he shakes his head at them.

"Wait, let me tell you about this chick. She was alright looking, but damn. I want romance, not hoe-mance. Check it out. I walked in, she saw I was a man, she practically fell to the bed, and lifted up her legs." Dean says exaggerating, as Jason looks at him with a smile. They all start laughing. Dean continues to mock, "She just dropped, and spread." He acts it out by lying back, and spreading his legs in the air.

"You're exaggerating." Jason states.

"No I'm not. She even had a condom taped to her ankle. It had a sign written next to it. If you can see this, use it. I'm tired of these easy ladies. I need something more. I need some love." Dean explains.

"Awww, my little baby is growing up. He's graduating to the next level." Daren states with a proud look on his face, as he reaches out to pinch Dean's cheeks. Dean pushes his hands away.

"Jason you need to learn from Dean, and stop teasing him." Daren states as he looks at Jason.

Jason looks at Dean funny. "Love huh? Yeah I can learn a lot from Dean."

Jason pauses for a second and then leans towards Dean. "So how was it?" he asks loud enough for all to hear.

The men start laughing slightly, and then get quiet to hear Dean's response. They all look at Dean. Dean sees them looking, but starts eating. He looks up, and they are still looking at him.

"Come on man. I don't know what you're talking about." Dean states and then looks away.

"How was it, Mr. I want romance?" Jason continues, as they all continue to pressure Dean.

"How was what? Eat your food and leave me alone." Dean states. Dean goes back to eating. He looks up and sees everyone still staring at him. "Ok, the pussy was good." He blurts out. And they all throw up their hands. They start laughing so loud that some of the people in the restaurant turn around to see what the loud laughter is about.

"Yeah, tell them about you and your latest chick." Dean states with vengeance.

"What? That had nothing to do with me, that was all her." Jason states.

"What happened? Daren asks. Tonka and Daren eagerly listen, being the only two that did not hear the story.

"I was with this fine Nubian Queen, from Queens. One thing led to another, and I found myself staring down some long spread legs. So I'm doing my thing. Sideways, regular, doggy style, and dropped a load in it, but only after she got hers of course." Jason states, but is interrupted.

"They all get theirs when you tell the story. I want to hear what the girls got to say about it." Dean states and they all start laughing.

"She'd be like, 'That guy promised me the world, and bust as soon as he touched it." Daren adds.

"Your mom's never complained. Now let me finish the story." Jason states, and then continued. "So I finished doing my thing, pulled out, and laid beside her. We talked for a few seconds about how good it was, and then I went to take the condom off. When I reached for it, the condom was not on my jimmy."

Dean is already laughing since he knows the story.

"What? You bust in her raw dog?" Daren asks concern, and knowing that was no joking matter. Each of them has felt the feeling of waiting on a pregnancy test from a chicken head you did not want to get pregnant.

"Naw, it wasn't that. It didn't break because the feeling would have become suddenly intense. Many times I have been up in something, and it was average, but all of a sudden it would get intense. I would know the condom broke, but it was not like that this time. I had it on when I came. So now I'm searching all over the place for the condom. I stripped the bed, and she felt inside of her, but we could not find it. She laid back on the bed talking about, 'that happens to me all the time.' I just wanted to find the condom. After checking under the bed, the closet, and the windowsill, she wanted to do it again. I couldn't do anything with her because I was obsessed with the condom. I eventually left her naked and frustrated." Jason states.

"You're crazy. Why didn't you use another condom?" Daren asks.

"I don't know. It just tripped me out losing a condom like that." Jason states.

"That is messed up, you're cheating on Tammy, and she's a good woman." Tonka states.

"Don't go there." Dean warns.

"Naw, it's ok. Y'all are my dogs." Jason states and then looks at Tonka. "Tammy and I broke up a week ago."

"What happened?" Daren asks.

"I caught her cheating with another man, at her apartment." Jason states sadly.

Everyone is surprise as they wait for Jason to tell them what happened.

This is something every man and woman hates to do. Tell their friends that their mate was cheating. It makes them feel inadequate, like they are not sexually capable of pleasing their mate.

"I came over to her apartment, and let myself in. I saw both man's and woman's clothing on the floor, leading to the bedroom. I heard music coming from the bedroom, and peeked in. I saw Tammy in bed kissing another man. I was about to barge in, but I saw some tacks on the refrigerator. I sprinkled the tacks on the floor by the bedroom door. I then went to the fuse box, and turned off all the fuses. I felt my way to the front door because it was dark. I rushed outside the front door, and listened by the door. I first heard a women screaming in pain, and then a man's voice screaming. I left and never came back." Jason explains.

"She did not deserve that. Tammy put up with a lot of your cheating." Daren states.

"Yes she did because she should have been more mature about it." Jason justifies.

They all stop and look at Jason.

"Mature? You have been cheating on her since you met her, and now she is trying to pay you back." Daren answers.

"Yeah, but she still could have handled the situation in a more mature fashion." Jason states.

"She knows you come over at that time, so she wanted to get caught. You messed up a good woman." Tonka states.

"Probably, but it's tacky to have sex with someone else, just to get your man back. I never thought her to be that kind of girl, so we are done. I have not heard from her yet, and it's been a week." Jason states.

She was wrong, in Jason's mind, no matter how many times he cheated on her. All he could comprehend is he caught her, and she was wrong. Despite the many times she forgave him, he would not forgive her. Go figure.

"She has not called you because she may be in the hospital." Dean states.

"Maybe, but I don't care. It's the single life for me, because there are more ladies in the sea." Jason says trying to put up a good front. "I'm single again, so halla at your boy."

14

"What do you mean again? You were always single." Daren says jokingly.

"I mean officially." Jason says.

Daren looks at them all.

"Now this is remarkable. You each remind me of myself, during the different stages in my love life. Tonka is the innocent stage, not really concerned about women, yet still they come around. Jason is in the, 'I'll screw everything phase.' That was my childish years." Daren states.

"Shut up." Jason states, realizing the insult.

"Don't worry brother, you will settle down and find love. We're praying for you. Dean is tired of screwing everyone he can, and is now looking for romance. Someday you will all end up married and happy. I hope."

CHAPTER TWO:
THE GIRLS

Daren's home is in a middle age, lower class neighborhood. He has lived there all his life. He has a two floor home with a basement. It's a lot of room for just two people, but they hope to have a family one day. They thought about renting out the basement, even though it's illegal; however, they value their privacy more then the extra money they could gained.

The home used to belong to Daren's parents, but they sold it to him, and retired to Florida. They put off their retirement for a year and a half, while waiting for Daren and his wife, Jennifer, to fix their credit. They left some of their furniture to Daren and Jennifer. "It's a good thing they had good taste," Jennifer would say to Daren, "Or we would have to throw everything out."

The home is neat and well kept. Daren and Jennifer have a tight budget, but they make do. She works as a teacher, and her school is only ten miles away from their home. The one car they have is used by her, because Daren works in Manhattan. It is easier for him to take public transportation, even though he hates it. He often complains about how he hates people squeezing against him on the bus.

Jennifer is an average looking women. She does not have the type of face that would make you say, "I got to get with that." But she is not ugly either. She has the type of face you would probably not recognize in a crowd. Her body is the same way. She has a nice body, don't get me wrong, but she covers it with baggy clothes. You'll see just enough up top to know she is a woman, no more, no less. Yeah she is average in every way, but as you get to know her, you can see how one might fall in love with her. Daren met Jennifer in college, and it was her who pursued him. Daren was in her class, and did not notice her. Jennifer would listen to how smart he was and how he expressed himself in class, and she slowly started to fall in love with him. She started conversations with him to feel him out. He was able to handle every topic she went into. One day Daren saw Jennifer talking to the teacher. She was wearing sweats as she usually did, but this time she had her hands in her pocket. This caused the back of the sweats to tighten, and to reveal the junk in her trunk. Needless to say, Daren was a fan of hers after that, and Jennifer could not figure out why. She did realized that Daren was just out for a booty call. She did not answer that call, but she expressed her deep love for him. She wanted him, but she told him she wanted to wait until she was married. She explained she was not a virgin, but wanted her wedding night to be some what special. She caught Daren's eyes with her statement. She was a good contrast to the girls who was giving it out like free cheese. He messed around on her a little in the beginning, until he fell in love with her. She knew how to get to his heart. She observed that he measured love by how much a person did for him. Jennifer would make his lunch, and eat it with him when she could. She would put his lunch in a bag, when he had to go to class. It just took a month for him to tell her he loved her. He did not say he loved her much after that. He only told her on birthdays, and special holidays, but he didn't have to say it all the time. Jennifer could see it in his eyes every time he looked at her. They had their arguments, but their love has never changed, throughout their six years of marriage.

Jennifer is talking with Carmen as they sit on the couch.

"So where is that crazy husband of yours?" Carmen asks.

"He is eating dinner with his friends. He should be home soon." Jennifer states as she starts smiling. "Don't worry about my man, worry about where Jose is. Living la vida loca."

She laughs, but Carmen does not. She frowns up a bit. "Child please, I'm living la vida nada. I got rid of him today." Carmen says.

Jennifer gives her that look as to say, "Here we go again." The look comes out in her voice. "Ok, what did he do?   He didn't buy you something, too cheap, or what? I know you like those men with money."

"Men today have no passion or maybe I have no passion for them." Carmen complains.

It is true. Carmen is an official gold digger. In fact, she is an instructor at the school of gold digging. Hood rats have been clocking her style for years. Wanting to pull the players she pulled, and wishing they had the looks she had.

Carmen has her own money though. That is something few people know. She got her money from a lawsuit. She was hit by a City bus, when she was younger. She was not a pretty child. She was over weight, but started losing weight just before puberty. Her weight lost was due to the bus accident. With a broken leg, most children gain weight, but Carmen lost her appetite. Puberty did her well. Her body developed nicely, and she started taking care of herself. By sixteen she was the most popular girl in high school, but she kept her old friends. One of which was Jennifer, who used to defend her against children who would tease her. She is now beautiful, and men approach her constantly. She loved the attention at first, but it soon became annoying. Every time she goes to the mall, she has to fight them off. She usually runs into at least three guys who want to have her baby, two guys who think they know her from some place, a guy who will swear his undying love for her, and a female who just gets down like that. She hates the fact they would tell her they love her, without even knowing her, but based on her beauty. She hates the fact that they never want to know the real her, but wants her body or to be seen with her. She would use some of them to get as much as she could from them. She calls it payback. If she finds a man she is attracted to, she might sleep with him, if he doesn't say or do something stupid.

Carmen does not sleep with too many men because being called a whore is not appealing to her. Some women say that men do it, so why can't we? Carmen does not carry this point of view.

"Yeah men do it, that's why we call them dogs." She would say. She did not view whoring as a women being bold, but found it sleazy. Some would argue that it is just as sleazy as using men for money, but it is not the same. Some women don't want to own up to this, but men don't want a whore or a loose woman. Sure they do when they want that fast ass on a Saturday night, but when they want to get married, they look for a decent woman. I know all the loose women are saying, "I'm going to do what I want to do regardless of what men think." Yeah they will say that, but what else can they say. Once you sleep with too many men, you can't erase it or take it back. Being called a whore is easy to get into, but hard as hell to get out of. You have to embrace it, or move to another place where they don't know you.

Carmen never thought about falling in love, especially at first sight. Especially to someone who didn't appear to have money. She was used to dealing with high rollers, but Tonka is not like that. Maybe she sees her old self in him, or maybe it was his teddy bear look. Who knows why we fall in love. Cupid does what he wants, when he wants. All Carmen know is she has it bad.

"I met someone today. Well I didn't meet him, but I gave him my number." Carmen states.

"What is he blinging? What is he rolling in, and how much doe he got? I know the drill." Jennifer asks.

"Ketchup." Carmen states with a look of admiration in her face. Jennifer looks at her with a puzzled look. "Ketchup what? Are you going to explain, or are you going to stay there with that goofy look on your face?" Jennifer asks.

"He had ketchup on the side of his mouth. He was eating and talking to his hamburger, and it was so cute and sexy. He looks like a cuddly teddy bear." Carmen says with excitement. "He was talking dirty to his food, and it got to me."

"You have liked guys before." Jennifer states.

"I know, but I'm really feeling this guy. I was pouring on the charm, and he didn't even pay me any attention. He looked annoyed I interrupted him eating." Carmen states.

Jennifer is staring at Carmen and smiling. "I have never seen you like this before. Are you in---"

"I don't know, but look at me. Just talking about him makes me smile. I have never been in love before, but here I am getting goose bumps over a man I never really met." Carmen states.

Jennifer thinks to herself, and then speaks. "Hold up. You said he was a big guy, and into his food? Where did you meet him?"

"At Joe's." Carmen replies with a puzzled look on her face. "Why?"

"He has long hair and looks a little Indian and Black mixed?" Jennifer asks

Carmen thinks to herself for a half a second. "Yeah, why?" She asks again.

"I know him. He is one of Daren's friends. His name is Tonka, and he may be with Daren right now." Jennifer states in amazement.

Carmen thinks for a few seconds, and then looks at Jennifer. "Double up?"

"You know it." Jennifer states. "Wait, Tonka is not rich."

"I'm not out for money. I want him." Carmen explains.

Jennifer looks at her. Carmen looks back at her.

"I'm for real. I have a feeling about this one." Carmen says.

"Tonka is not going to be that easy to crack. I have not seen him with too many ladies, and the few that I did see him with, did not last long."

"I'll crack him." Carmen says with a scheming look on her face. "The way he was eating that burger, he got to be good. You know my motto. To get downtown, you have to go downtown."

Carmen and Jennifer both laugh. "I know you're good, but I don't think you're hearing me. Tonka's idea of downtown is his stomach. Tonka will not be easy." Jennifer states.

"I know men. I'll have him eating out of my plate before you know it."

"Naw. That is the easy part. The trick is to eat out of his plate. His mother doesn't even eat out of his plate." Jennifer jokes.

"I will be eating out of his plate the first night we go out. I have to pull all my tricks out for this one, but something tells me he's a keeper." Carmen states.

"I am warning you do not eat out of his plate. He will stick you with his folk. Daren told me that Tonka did that to someone before."

"You know I got this. How many times have you seen me fail?" Carmen asks proudly.

Jennifer looks out at her yard.

"Well if you're so good, can you tell me how to get this man to clean up the front yard?" Jennifer states jokingly.

"A piece of cake. You got a CD. player and some anthem music?" Carmen asks.

"Yeah." Jennifer answers.

CHAPTER THREE:
THE MEETING

After leaving the dinner, Jason and Dean are headed home to Brooklyn. On the train they decide to venture into Manhattan. Dean knows of a good cake place near his job. It also gives them time to talk in person because the phone is not the same. The two are the closest of the four friends. They have known each other the longest, since they grew up on the same block. They met Tonka when they were ten years old. He lived two blocks away from them, and used to play on their block. In High school they all met Daren, who acted older then them, but was cool. Three good friends is a lot for a person to have, so they each considered themselves blessed.

"I'm full, but there is always room for cake." Jason states as he is rubbing his stomach. "Eating with the guys was fun. We need to eat out more often."

"Anytime is good for me, but getting us all together is hard." Dean responds. He suddenly stops and points to a tall building. "I work right there in that tall building. The same building my dream lady works in."

"Why didn't you talk to her? That is not like you." Jason asks, remembering the player Dean used to be.

"The elevator was too crowded, and I was thrown off by her beauty. It's love at first sight." Dean states as they discuss such a personal topic, while walking down such a busy street.

"The next time you see her, approach her. You know how we do. You got to represent man." Jason states, trying to encourage him.

"I can't just walk up to her like that. This is love, not some girl in the club I'm trying to screw." Dean states. "I'm going to say something to her, but it has to be right."

"Hey what's up with your apartment?"

Jason strategically changes the subject, not wanting Dean to try to convince him of how he had to wait for the right time. Jason thinks Dean will never get to talk to his dream girl, if he waits for the right time. The right time may never come. He does not want to say that to Dean because Dean will stubbornly argue the point. It is something Dean has done many times in the past.

"I still have to be out by next week." Dean replies.

"You can always stay with me if you need a place." Jason offers.

"Thanks, but I will find something I like." Dean states. He starts to say something else, but he stops walking, and stares ahead. Jason walks a few steps ahead of him, but comes back when he notices Dean has stopped walking.

"What's up with you?" Jason asks puzzled.

"There she is. She must have been working late." Dean barely states. Jason looks at how nervous Dean is and knows that is why he can't talk to her.

Walking towards them, with her briefcase, is the finest girl in the world. Her hair is out, and is shoulder length. She is five feet, ten inches, with a fat butt, and a nice size chest. Her brown complexion is accented by her brown eyes, and hair. She has on a brown sweater, with a long skirt, and boots.

"Dam, she is fine. Talk to her." Jason urges.

"I'm not ready." Dean argues as the lady comes closer to them.

"You're never going to be ready." Jason states, but she has passed them already. Jason reaches out and taps her shoulder. Dean watches in shock.

"Excuse me miss, my friend wants to ask you something." Jason states as he points to Dean. Jason knows it sounds childish, but he had to do something to help Dean.

The problem becomes worse when the lady replies. "Save your silly jokes. I'm not a child, and I don't have time for childish games."

She looks at Jason first, and then at Dean. Dean knows he had to say something then and there. If he didn't she would never take anything he said, seriously.

"Please excuse my friend, but I assure you this is no game, and I am no child. I have seen you before in that building over there, where I work." Dean states as he starts moving closer to her. Jason walks away from them. He knew Dean did not like it when he hung around. Dean would always say it throws off his game.

"I work there too." She states.

Dean smells her perfume, and he knows that smell will forever be etched in his mind. He could not place the perfume, but he knew he had smelled it before. He can not believe he was this close to her. She is even more adorable then he had thought. Being this close to her makes his stomach tingle, but to his surprise, he keeps his composure.

"I don't want to take up your time. I was just wondering can I make you mines."

Dean stated and then stares real hard at her. "Excuse me were you born this beautiful or did you have to work at it?" Dean states charmingly.

Dawn smiles at the comment.

"Hey. It was a corny, but dependable line, which got a good response." Dean thinks.

"What's your name?" Dean asks as if finding out her name would give him magical powers over her.

"Oh a name, what's in a name, for a rose is a rose just the same?" She sings out.

"This is a bad sign" Dean thinks to himself. "She does not want to give me her name. If she liked me, I would have her name already, but I can't give up."

Dawn mistakes his silence for ignorance, and thinks her words went right over his head. She thinks to herself, "If he asks me what I'm talking about, I'm leaving."

She notices the pause and asks, "What's your name?"

"Shakespeare." he says, as she laughs.

"Tussah. OK Shakespeare, what's your last name?" she asks being humorous.

"Love." Dean states.

She smiles and asks, "And who gave you such a prestigious last name?"

"Cupid gave it to me the first time I saw you." Dean answers with a serious look. She starts to stare at him seriously, but blushes a little.

"My mother always said Cupid is Stupid." Dawn states as she looks at Dean half serious.

"No, he got this one right." Dean replies.

Dean wants to look over at Jason because he knows Jason is cheering him on, but he does not want her to see him looking at Jason, and to think this is a game.

"Love huh? You hardly know me, so how can you love me?" she asks rhetorically.

Dean looks deep into the oceans of her eyes. "I don't know how, that is Cupid's job. All I know is I do." Dean states.

"Love?" She says shaking her head a little, and smiling slightly. "You don't love me, but you would love to get into my pants I bet."

Abort Dean's mind tells his brain. This is going down hill because you have touched upon a pet peeve of hers. The mind sends a message to the legs to start walking. He also sends a message to the mouth to say something degrading about her, as he walks away. The mind feels we have to keep out ego in tact. The heart tells Dean's legs not to move. The mind questions the hearts authority, but the heart argues that he too is a major organ. The legs listen to the heart. That is all love is, an argument between the heart and the mind. Sometimes the heart wins, and sometimes the mind wins. Sometimes they tie; sometimes they agree.

"I don't know what guy did you in, but I am not that guy. My name is Dean." Dean states.

"Yeah and I guess you don't tell lies, like the other men." She says.

"Yeah I do lie, which I should have done when I first met you."

Dean states and is shocked he said it. Dawn is shocked as well, but Dean keeps going.

"Men lie because women can't handle the truth." Dean states. He knows it is not the right thing to say, but he figures he has nothing to lose.

"Now that is cute and original." She states.

"Well I just told you the truth, and you didn't believe me." Dean argues.

"Well I have a boyfriend, so it doesn't really matter." She lies, as she walks away.

"What about a friendship?" Dean yells behind her.

"A friendship? So you don't want to have sex with me?" She asks.

"I do but----" Dean states, but it is too late. She is walking away.

She pauses for a second, and then states without looking back, "I have too many friends already."

Jason walks over to him.

"What happened? Go after her." Jason encourages.

Dean runs after her. "Excuse me miss." As Dawn turns around frustrated.

"What now. Look I will call the police." She states with her cell phone in her hand.

"That did not come out right. Look the truth is I want you. You're beautiful, but I am interested in knowing the inner you. I love you. I have seen you in our building, and I think you're the most beautiful person I have ever seen or ever will see." Dean states honestly.

"That is good and all, but I am not interested. I just don't feel you like that." Dawn states as she walks off again.

"You don't know me." Dean lobs the ball to her.

"Exactly." She states as she hits the ball out of the park.

Dean looks at her walk away. "You're not even wearing pants." He yells behind her.

Jason walks over to him.

"What happen? I did not see her give you a number." Jason asks, as he is still trying to see where she went.

"No, she blew me off." Dean states not wanting to look in the direction the lady walked in.

"What did you say?" Jason asks.

"I told her I love her." Dean confesses.

"Aw man. You know better than that." Jason says as he throws up his hands. "Never tell them you love them is number one in the player's rule book. That gives them the upper hand."

"It's not about the game anymore. It's about love. I love her, and I don't know what to do about it." Dean complains.

"Come on, I'll buy you a drink." Jason states.

"You know I don't like to drink."

"I was talking about milk and cookies."

CHAPTER FOUR:
A MAN'S EGO

Daren is walking home. He waves to a few neighbors across the street. He walks a little further, and sees this old man dressed in a black suit. The old man looks like the man who dances for the Great Adventure commercials. Daren stares at him, expecting him to start dancing.

"Do it old man, come on." Daren says looking at him. The old man stares at him, and then walks away.

Daren continues walking down the street. Just before he gets to his yard, he hears anthem music. Jennifer and Carmen are at the window playing it, but Daren does not see them. Daren stops and starts tapping his foot.

"You sure this will work." Jennifer asks from inside the house.

"As long as it is anthem music, it will appeal to their ego." Carmen states as she is peeking out the window.

"Why so many rakes?" Jennifer asks.

"Because other men will join in. It's like the music bonds with their testosterone, and they have to work together. Just watch." Carmen states as she peeks out the window. The anthem music is heard playing.

Daren is still tapping his foot. He sees the rakes, takes one, and starts raking the yard to the music. A Hindu man in a suit is passing by.

He is taken in by the music, and starts tapping his foot. He enters the yard and starts helping him. A boy on a bike is riding, but drops his bike, grabs a broom, and starts sweeping. They are all lured by the music, and are cleaning to it. A guy walks by in a tight shirt, and pom-pom shorts. He is switching. He walks by as he looks at the window where the music is coming from. The ladies turn up the music trying to get him.

"Don't even try that with me ladies." Gary responds, as he continues to walk down the street. The ladies just wave their hands at him. The men and the boy are oblivious to what is going on around them. They act as a team, as one holds the garbage bag, and the other two rake in the leaves. The yard is finished in no time.

"You are a genius. How did you learn this?" Jennifer asks.

"A trick my aunt taught me." Carmen states.

Jennifer looks at her proudly. "Maybe you can eat from Tonka's plate." Jennifer states.

"Now don't let on that you made him clean the yard. Let him think it is his idea. Men like to think they are in control, and a part of controlling them is letting them believe they are in control." Carmen tells her.

The yard is completed, and the men are still tapping their feet. The music stops, and it seems like the spell is broken. The boy looks at the men as to say, "I don't know you." The boy gets on his bike, and rides off. Daren looks at the man with him and they stare at each other for a few seconds, and politely nod to each other. The man picks up his brief case, and leaves. Daren comes inside.

"Wow, that is some good music." He says as he enters the door. "Hi dear." He says and is about to kiss her, but he sees Carmen. "Hi, oh yeah Carmen? I met a friend of yours today. A guy you left your number with. Boy I tell you, you get around."

"Shut up. You're so stupid. I know you know him, because Jennifer already told me. We're double dating on Saturday." Carmen says laughing.

"I already told him Friday, but I can change it." Daren states.

"What is your friend like?" Carmen asks trying to gain some insight in how to get to Tonka's heart.

"He is a simple guy, not stupid, but basic. He likes the simple things in life. Just don't mess with his food, and he will tolerate you." Daren warns.

"I don't want to be tolerated." Carmen shoots back with pride. "I wanna be loved."

"Honey, she thinks she can eat out of his plate." Jennifer says. "I think she can do it."

"That is a no-no. You will lose a finger, literally. I have seen it." Daren says and turns to Jennifer. "Remember Cindy Lewis, that old school friend I saw on the street a year ago. Remember her hand." Daren curls up his hand and holds it close to his body.

Jennifer thinks for a while. "Oh damn." She says as she screws up her face like she just ate a lemon. "That was Tonka?" Daren nods yes. Carmen is watching and getting a little nervous.

"You're exaggerating, right. I have charm, and that goes a long way." Carmen says unsure. "Right?"

"She does have skills when it comes to men." Jennifer tries to encourage her friend, thinking about how Carmen got the men to rake the yard. After all, she has seen Carmen make a man give her five hundred dollars for an abortion she never had, and a baby she never had; have the man accuse her of lying, then give her another five hundred for even thinking she was lying. Yeah Carmen is good.

"Scheme and plan what you will, but if you reach in his plate, we will be spending the evening in the emergency room." Daren warns.

CHAPTER FIVE:
THE ELEVATOR

Dean is getting in a freight elevator at the fortieth floor. He knows Dawn works late sometimes, and does not want to run into her on the elevator. Most of the people have gone home for the day. On the thirty fifth floor, the girl of his dreams, Dawn, gets on the elevator. She sees Dean and is startled. She is used to having the freight elevator to herself. She started taking the service elevator in the day, because it is quicker. Sometimes she would see service men on it, and they would make her take the other elevators, but that was rare. Dawn knows the passenger elevators are empty, but she is in the habit of taking the freight elevator.

She sees Dean, continues in the elevator, turns around, and looks straight ahead. Dawn is not going to let him chase her away.

Dean is thinking he should say something, but Dawn keeps looking straight. He does not feel like getting disrespected again.

Dawn is hoping Dean will not say speak to her. She wishes she would not have got on the elevator, but she does not want to appear like she had to cower away from Dean. All she has to do is stand there and look at the elevator door for a few seconds. After all, the elevator is fast.

"Why did I have to stay late and work on the Kent project." She thinks to herself. "I know I should have gone home, but I just had to stay here. Awwww, what is that smell." Dawn frowns up her face, but does not look back. "I hope that is the elevator, and not his breath. Wait, I know I didn't fart, and his breath can't smell like that. It has to be the elevator."

Dean looks around nervously. "Damn that slipped out. I would have never done that, but I usually have the elevator alone. How was I to know she was going to get on? I just had to volunteer to close up the pharmacy. I would have been out of here by now. Forget this punk stuff. I'm going to say something." Dean thinks. He goes to say something to her, and the elevator suddenly stops. Dean and Dawn both look around, and wait for a few seconds for the elevator to start up again. When it does not, Dawn starts pressing buttons.

"What's going on?" Dawn states as she is looking around nervously. "I don't like small spaces."

When she was younger, she once got herself locked in an old refrigerator that was sitting out for the garbage. She screamed for what seemed like hours, but no one answered. She did not know that the same thing that kept the cool air in also muffled her screams from the outside world. The darkness of the refrigerator made her mishap even more frightening. The louder she screamed, the quieter was her silence. She pushed on the door, but this old refrigerator could not be push open from the inside. Years ago, many children died in abandoned refrigerators, just like this one. It was against the law to throw one of these old refrigerators out, without taking the door off. The owner didn't care when he left it in front of the abandoned building. He cared about as much, as little Dawn knew it was unsafe. But there she was, banging on the door for her life. That day was hot, but it felt cold inside the clammy refrigerator. Dawn banged on the door hoping someone would hear. She hugged herself franticly. Crying enough to flood the refrigerator, had she not ran out of tears. Her eyes were dried up by her loss of liquid. Her only break from fear is hatred. Hatred usually overrules the other emotions, but they say love conquers all. There she was, in the darkness, hating the person who had caused all this. Suddenly she heard a voice from the outside call out to her.

"Are you OK? You're going to be alright." Dean states, trying to comfort the frantic Dawn.

Dawn jumps at the sound of his voice, and comes back to reality. She looks around her at the elevator, and starts breathing heavily. "I got to get out of here." She states as she starts banging on the elevator door.

"The emergency light is on, so there must be some kind of power failure." Dean states, as he moves Dawn away from the door. He presses the emergency button, but hears no response. He looks at his cell phone, and looks for a signal, but it has no bars. Dawn sees him, and checks hers, but there are no bars.

"It's going to be ok. We are fine." He states with enough confidence to reassure Dawn, who looks at him, and is shaking her head in agreement.

"Yeah we're going to be fine, just don't leave me alone." Dawn says, and she comes close to him.

Dean looks around as to say, "where can I go." He realizes that Dawn is having some sought of emotional distress. He takes her by the shoulders and looks into her eyes. "I will not let anything happen to you. I swear it. The most that could have happened is a black out. This elevator is wide, and has strong cables. It is not about to fall. If it was a terrorist attack, we would be dead already. Just relax. I got you." Dean states.

Dawn looks at him and believes in what he says. Dean sits down and Dawn sits down right next to him.

"For a second, I was in that refrigerator again." Dawn states with a blank stare on her face.

"What do you mean?"

"I can't tell you about it, because it's something that happened to me when I was younger." Dawn states.

"Why can't you tell me? Is it that personal?" Dean asks.

'Yeah and I don't know you like that."

"Tell me your name." Dean states.

"Dawn, why?"

"Hi Dawn, I am Dean. There, we know each other." Dean jokes.

"Yeah, right, now I can tell you my most inner secrets." Dawn states sarcastically.

"I see you're returning to your old self. " Dean says, as Dawn laughs.

"Tell me what happened to you when you. It's better to tell a stranger, besides, talking is good therapy. Look how calm you are." Dean says, looking into her face. In his mind he is looking at how her long hair crosses her face. He thinks that if he is to die, it would be alright, because he has seen the most beautiful girl in the world.

"I can't do it with you staring in my grill." Dawn states with a little smile.

"Ok. We will turn back to back, that way you can't see my face." Dawn shakes her head because he could not believe she was doing this. They move to the center of the elevator, and lean on each other's back. Dawn takes a few seconds to talk.

37

"I can't believe I'm telling you this because I have never told this story to anyone. On a nice sunny day, my father was taking me to the zoo. He did not live with me and my mother, and had very little money. My mother gave him some money to take me to the zoo. He took me around the corner, and told me he would be back. He left me playing with a friend I knew, while he most likely went to a bookie. My friend and I played until her mother called her in to eat. I kept playing outside because there were no children to play with. The street had a few abandoned houses, so there were not too many people passing by. I ended up, accidentally, locking myself in an old refrigerator, and could not get out. I screamed and banged on the door, but no one came for a long time. I don't know how long I was in there, but it felt like hours. My friend finally heard me, and got her father. Her father let me out. Since then, it seems like I live my life out of an old refrigerator. Sometimes feeling free, sometimes feeling shut in. Mostly shut in though. I hate it." Dawn states as she looks over in his direction. "You know what I mean?"

"No, because no one can know exactly what you mean, except for God; however, I feel what you're saying." Dean states. He thinks for a second. "What happened when your mother found out?"

"She never found out because I did not tell her. She would have never let me see him again. When he came back, I never told him what had happened, and I was not even disappointed when he said he lost the money to go to the zoo. I loved him unconditionally, and he was never able to build up an ounce of love for me, or at least any love I could perceive."

"What ever happened to your father?"

"I don't know. I always assumed he was dead. One day he just stopped coming by."

"Have you ever tried to look for him?"

"For what? A child should never have to search for their father. Why should I find him anyway, just to curse him out?"

Dawn is tearing, and Dean senses it. His first instinct is to turn around and hold her, but he does not. Facing her might make her embarrassed she is crying. He sees her hair lying on his shoulder, and starts to run his hand through it. Dawn notices it and does nothing. He then reaches his hands over and start running his fingers through her hair, but closer to the scalp. It relaxes Dawn as she leans her head back more. Dean stops, and then goes to his bag. Dawn is looking to see what he is doing.

"I'm so stupid. I have a radio on my Mp3." Dean says as he pulls the Mp3 out of his bag. He puts on one of the headphones, and Dawn puts on the other. He tunes the radio and noise is heard. He searches the stations, and finally gets an AM. news station to come in fairly clear. They both tune into the radio, and hear there is a statewide blackout. They also have no idea how long it will last.

"I'm getting thirsty." Dawn states.

"It hasn't even been a half an hour and you're dying of thirst." Dean jokes.

"I was thirsty before I left the office." Dawn states.

Dean pulls out a large, half empty water bottle, and offers it to her.

"Let's save it." She says as she looks at it funny. Dean notices the look.

"You just don't want to drink after me." Dean states.

"I don't know you well enough."

39

"Fine, you will want some after a few hours because it's getting hot in here." Dean states.

"I'll be OK." Dawn says.

Hours later, Dean and Dawn are like they are old friends. They are both sweating, but Dean has his shirt off.

"I am thirty two years old, and I was born in Atlanta, but moved to N.Y. when I was five. My mother is the only family I have, and she lives in Jamaica, Queens. She hardly ever visits me, but I see her when I can." Dawn states.

"I am thirty five, and I'm a native New Yorker. I have two brothers and a sister, but they do not live in N.Y. any longer. My mother is in North Carolina, so I am all alone in this big City." Dean states. "Where do you live?"

"I live here in Manhattan, and you?" She asks.

"I live in Brooklyn, but not for long. I –" Dean pauses. He thinks for a second. "Dang it,"

"What happened?" Dawn asks.

"I had an appointment to see an apartment this evening. They were going to hold it, but I guess that is lost. They said it has to be rented by tomorrow. I need to find a place to live." Dean explains.

"They will hold it because of the black out." Dawn states.

"No they won't." They other people have already seen the apartment, and just have to call them to say yes."

"Why do you need a new apartment? You can't pay your rent." Dawn states as she shoots him a smile.

"Oh ok. I see you're feeling more relaxed now huh? I see you got jokes. That is Black on Black stereotyping, when you see a Black man, and already you assume he can't pay his rent." Dean states in his militant voice. "No, I paid my rent, but I got in an argument with the owner, and he wants me out. My lease was up last week, and I absolutely have to be out next week."

"You're a trouble maker huh? A brawler?"

"No, not at all."

Two more hours passes as their friendship strengthens. There are basically three types of friendships. The friends you can say you met. Either you met them in school, work, or through another friend, but the point is you meet them. You may not remember the day or month, but most can remember the year.

Then there are the friends that you never remember meeting. You just knew them all your life. Every since you can remember, they have been there, just like an older sibling.

Then there are those bonds that are initiated by a crisis. Most friendships are made over time, but the trial friendship is made by the seriousness of the crisis. For example, there are a few people who became good friends because they helped each other through the 911 incident. These friendships are formed fast and hard, depending on how much your life is in danger.

Dean and Dawn spent a couple of hours forging their crisis friendship. The bonds form twice as fast as a regular friendship would have, and sometimes grow twice as strong. When you think of it, all friendships are made strong through crisis situations. Sure, through time you get to know someone better, but when you help a friend that needs you, it deepens the relationship.

"So she kept telling the joke, and I laughed so hard I wet myself. And that is my most embarrassing moment." Dawn states.

"Yuk, you're nasty." Dean states as he frowns his face at the thought.

"I told you it was gross." Dawn tries to explain, but she knows Dean is just messing with her.

"I bet they teased you afterwards. Pissy Dawn, Pissy Dawn." Dean sings to her.

"They did not." Dawn protests.

"They probably made up a nursery rhyme after you. You had better be good, and not laugh too hard or pissy Dawn is going to get you." Dean jokes.

"You see, this is why I don't like to share with people." Dawn states with a smile.

"So when did this happened, yesterday?" Dean asks jokingly.

"No, silly, when I was fourteen." Dawn states as she reaches for Dean's water bottle, and starts drinking it.

"Our first kiss." Dean states and he watches Dawn drink.

"What?" Dawn states and looks at him. "You wish."

"What nothing. Our lips have touched on the bottle." Dean explains.

"It's not the same." Dawn says smiling at him.

"Hey don't drink too much of that. I don't want you to turn into Pissy Dawn up in here." Dean teases.

"Shut up, stupid." Dawn thinks to herself. "Hey, what about you stinking up the elevator?"

"I told you that slipped out, and how was I to know you were getting on the elevator.' Dean states.

"You had the elevator smelling like year old diapers." Dawn teases.

42

Dean starts rocking his leg, and stands up. "I need a bathrooms; I have to go." Dean states as he looks around to see where he can go.

"Now who is going to wet his pants? Pissy Dean, Pissy Dean." Dawn states as she starts shaking up the last of the water. The sound makes Dean start to rocking even harder.

"Stop it. You're making it worse." Dean states as he keeps looking around.

Dawn finishes the last of the water, and hands Dean the bottle. Dean takes it and then looks at her.

"What type of men have you been dating? I can't use this. The hole is way too small."

Dean looks around and sees a panel. He opens it up, and sees a latch that releases the elevator doors. He opens the elevator doors, and sees he is in between floors. He tries to get the floor doors to open, but they do not.

"I can go right here. I won't get any in the elevator. "Dean states. He looks back at Dawn. "Now stand back, I don't want to hit you with this."

"Yeah right." Dawn laughs. "You don't want me to hurt my eyes straining to see it."

Dean goes and then turns to Dawn. "You have to go before I close it."

"No, I'm good. It is hot in here." Dawn states as she hopelessly tries to fan herself with her hand.

"Take off your top; you have a bra on." Dean suggests.

"You wish." Dawn states as she looks at him.

"A bra is like a bikini top. It does not turn me on in the least. Plus you don't know how long we will be here." Dean states trying to encourage her.

Dawn looks at him, but then accepts his reasoning. She takes off her top, and has an old looking bra on.

Dean starts laughing. "You have on one of those Grandma bras. I though you would have on something sexy, from Victoria secrets." Dean teases.

Dawn looks at him. "Stop it. This is not a grandma bra"

"You should take off you pants as well, it will be cooler." Dean states.

"You're pushing it now." Dawn states.

"Hey, I got to try."

Dawn thinks for a while, as she looks at Dean to see if he is staring at her in her bra. She sees he is paying her no extra attention.

"Did you mean it the other day?" Dawn asks.

"What?" Dean asks back.

Dawn looks away, and then looks back at him. "When you said you love me, it felt like you meant it." Dawn says seriously. "Men are always saying things to get into my pants."

Men are horny, Dawn is fine, and so Dean concludes she must get approached constantly. Men probably nag her all day. She has to fight them off at work, on the street, and on the train. It is understandable that she would not believe Dean when he stated he loved her. Dean looks at her as sincere as he can.

"No, I meant it. How did it make you feel when I said it?" He asks.

"I have been told that by many men, but when I thought about it later, I felt you were telling the truth. Something in the way you looked at me said you were real. Then I thought, how could you love me, and you don't know me." Dawn explains.

"I don't know you, but I want to know you. I want to know your thoughts and fears. What makes you cry and what puts a smile on your face? I want to know what scares you and what gives you goose bumps. I want to know how your face looks at night and how messy your hair can get. I want to know how your breath smells in the morning and I want to smell your personal body scent. I want to know your favorite position and what do you do when you're aroused. Do you moan, grit your teeth, scream, scratch, or all of the above. I want to know will I still love you this much when we are ninety years old, or will I love you even more; however, right now, I just know how I feel about you." Dean explains.

"But how can you, if you don't know how the person is on the inside. The inside is what counts. I want men to see the inside of me." Dawn states.

"How can I if you don't let me get close enough." Dean answers.

"How can I let them get close, if they are always trying to get into my pants?" Dawn asks.

"I'm not trying to get into your pants now am I?" Dean asks.

"Because we are stuck in an elevator." Dawn states.

"Oh yeah, the elevator, people would never do something here? We only have privacy and a floor." Dean says sarcastically.

Dawn looks at him as to say, "OK. You got me there." She thinks for a while with her head down, and then states, "Have you been in love before?"

"Not really, just some puppy love, but nothing like this." Dean states.

"I was once. He was a childhood friend. Blue was his name, and he would always protect me. He once jumped in the way to protect me from a vicious dog. We were best friends for a long time before we dated. I have never had a friend like that again, but I want one like that again. He was my first. One of two men I have slept with." Dawn states with sadness in her voice.

"How was your first time?" Dean asks. "I mean was it painful or were you excited?"

Dawn looks at him strangely. "Why would you want to know about that?" Dawn asks.

"I just like asking ladies about their first. Some say different things."

"My first time was painful, but I wanted to satisfy blue, so I endured it. It took me three times to start to like it enough to tolerate it. I could not believe, at first, that people enjoyed this." Dawn states.

"So what happened to Blue or are you with him now?" Dean asks trying to feel out his competition.

"No, he died about fifteen years ago." Dawn states.

"What happened?"

"Another boy liked me, and was constantly asking me out. I told him I had a man, and he became jealous. He tried to kill me one day, but Blue jumped in the way, and got it in the head." Dawn states. Dawn starts crying, and Dean puts his arm around her.

"I miss him so. I have never had another male friend like that. Now men don't want to protect you, they want to disrespect you. All they want is what is in your pants." Dawn states.

Dean finishes her sentence, "Get into your pants. Do me a favor and stop saying that please. I love you and will always want to be more then just friends. I want what is in your pants, but also what is in your mind and heart."

"Friendship is all I have to offer you. Sometimes it's more important than love. Can you be my friend?"

"I can do that, but I can't see how it is more important than love." Dean states.

"How can he get so close without touching? It is like telling a hungry man to smell and touch the food, but don't eat it." Dean thinks to himself.

"I met someone today, that is another reason why we can only be friends." Dawn explains as she gains Dean's full attention.

"Really, I thought you had a boyfriend?" Dean asks.

"Naw, I just said that for you to leave me alone." Dawn states. "I met this guy during lunch time, and I am very attracted to him. He plays for the NY. Giants. His name is Barry Banks. He is so fine." Dawn states.

Dean takes all of this in, and says, "Great. That is just what I want to hear. You like another man, who may be the best running back in Giants history. How did you meet him? Never mind, I don't want to know."

"I'm just saying I have someone I want to be with, but I need a different type of love. You have been a good friend to me already, and I don't want to loose that. I feel you can be another Blue to me." Dawn states.

Dean looks puzzled, and he states, "But you and Blue were dating."

"Yeah, but I need friendship right now. Can you be there for me? I promise to be there for you." Dawn states.

"But I might try something with you that you don't want me to try." Dean states.

"Like what, a kiss? We can get that out the way right now." Dawn says as she faces him.

"What? Kiss you now?" Dean asks.

"Right here, right now. Make a believer out of me. Sweep me off my feet. Show me the stars." Dawn says as she stands to her feet. Dean stands up and looks her in the eyes. He can not believe she is serious, but he does feel a sense of closeness with her. Dean puts his arms around her.

"I love you." Dean states.

"I know. I can feel it in your arms." Dawn replies.

Dean looks into her eyes. This is his one time shot at winning her over. He tries to focus all of his energy into his lips to transfer it to her. Dean leans over and kisses her with his tongue. His lips run smoothly over hers. Dean can not believe this is happening. He is kissing the girl he loves, and it is incredible. Her lips are soft and smooth as their tongues dance in their mouths. Dean wonders is he dreaming, and praises the blackout that made this possible. Dawn pulls away, and Dean reaches forward for one more swirl of the tongue. Dawn backs away again.

"That is enough tiger." Dawn states.

Dean has his eyes still closed, as he sits back down. Dawn sits down also.

"That was good. You have the softest lips, but there are no sparks." Dawn states.

"There were for me." Dean states.

"Now that the sensual part is behind us, can we be friends?" Dawn asks.

"I guess so. Whatever." Dean states.

She could have asks anything and he would have said yeah. He is whipped, like whip cream. He had made it a point in the past to feel nothing for a girl, and if he did, never, under any circumstances, show it. This is different. This is something he could not front about because it is too strong. He didn't care how it made him look. He is like the crack head of love. Just like a crack head forsakes all to follow crack, he would forsake all for her love. That is all that matters to him.

"We should try to get some sleep. There is no telling how long this will last." Dawn states as she looks tired.

"Sleep, at 12 AM." Dean states.

Dawn lies on Dean's stomach, and then gets off of it real quick.

"Is it OK. for me to lie on your stomach? I need a pillow." She asks.

Dean is happy she felt comfortable to do it first, without asking. "It's cool." He states. Dawn lies down and closes her eyes. She seems comfortable. Dean puts his arm around her.

"Even your stomach is soft. This is so comfortable." Dawn smiles to herself.

"My protector." She states.

"Hey, how come you don't want to be friends with the Barry?" Dean asks.

"I have learned to separate the two, because I can never have them together. I really believe you love me, and will care for me. There is nothing more powerful to me then friendship. Remember that Dean." Dawn explains.

"If you had a choice between friendship and love, which would you choose?" Dean asks.

"Friendship hands down. My love is physical, but my friendship is the type that is death until we part." She states.

"That is a shame." Dean states.

"What?"

"You're so beautiful that people never get to see the inside of you." Dean compliments her.

"Oh stop it. Which would you choose?" Dawn asks.

"Love, but it would be that old fashioned love where the person loves you for what's inside. That is how I love." Dean explains.

"We will see. Men have been claiming to love me ever since I came of age. Only one saw the inside of me." Dawn states.

"Sounds like you don't believe in love."

"I don't. I mean it's there, but it's hard to find or define." Dawn states.

"Then where does that leave Barry?" Dean asks.

"That is nothing but lust and fireworks. I just met him." Dawn explains. 'He makes me tingly inside, and that is apart of love to me. As for the friendship part, we will have to see how Barry does."

Dawn closes her eyes, and Dean stares into the elevator ceiling. He is deep in thought about the conversation they just had. He must try to understand her, if he is to win her heart.

Dawn falls to sleep immediately, and Dean follows afterwards. He is not really comfortable, but he does not want to wake Dawn.

Hours pass as they are in a deep sleep. Watching them there, one would think they are friends from childhood. The elevator suddenly jumps as the power comes on. Dawn looks around because she does not know where she is at first. When she realizes it, she gets happy, but Dean does not seem surprised.

"The power's back on." Dawn states.

"Thank God." Dean states as they both stand up, and Dean presses the button for the first floor. Dawn puts on her shirt.

"What time is it?" Dawn asks.

"2:56 AM. and I am starving."

"Let me treat you to breakfast. I know a place that might be open." Dawn states, but then thinks about it. "I don't know though because of the black out, but we might can find a place."

"Sounds good to me." Dean states.

They arrive on the first floor, and walk out the building. They see the Janitor, who looks at them strangely.

"I did not know people were stuck on the freight elevator. We got the people on the regular elevator off. No one is supposed to be on the freight elevator." The Janitor states more afraid they are going to report him for his negligence. They looked at him, and keep walking. Dawn takes Dean's arm as they walk out. They know he is negligent, but tonight is not a night of yelling and screaming at people. They have found a new friendship in each other, so no one is going to get in trouble tonight.

Dean and Dawn found a few restaurants were open. The owners were stranded there, and were watching over their business. When the lights came on, they decided to open up because a few people were out walking around.

Dean and Dawn are surprised to see how friendly people are, and how many people are out getting something to eat. Dean and Dawn find a quiet restaurant, and sit in the back at a table for two.

"I never thought food would taste this good." Dean says as he savors the first few bites of his pancakes.

"Do you regret our time in the elevator?" Dawn asks. It is sort of an insecure question, because she knows how much he cares for her. Secretly she likes the attentions he gives her. She feeds off of it, like a fire feeds off of fuel. Dawn admires her new friend, and feels she has found someone who will look out for her. Dean knows he has found his true love, but she does not feel the same way towards him. The two keep playing off of each others emotions, but we will see how long this all will last.

"No, because I was able to talk to you." Dean states.

"I accept." Dawn states out of the blue. Dean looks puzzled.

"What?" Dean asks. He starts thinking back, wondering if he missed something in the earlier conversation.

"When you offered me your friendship, I accept." Dawn states and she comes up from eating her waffles, and look at him to see his response.

"Well, I'm not offering it anymore." Dean states with a grin.

"Stop it silly." Dawn laughs, but is looking him in the eyes.

"What's that?" Dean asks as he looks at her.

"What's what?"

"The way you're looking at me feels like more then just a friend." Dean states with hope in his eyes. He thinks he sees something in her stare, but maybe he is wrong.

"Just pure unadulterated friendship." Dawn states.

"Well we can put some adultery in there somewhere." Dean states jokingly.

Dawn laughs a little, but continues, "I'm amazed at our friendship because it feels like we have known each other for years. I'm amazed I was in my bra around you, but you made me feel that comfortable." Dawn states while looking at him with admiration. "Come sit over here with me." Dawn says as she moves over. Dean comes over to her side, not even thinking about his plate. Dean sits next to her, and she lies gently on his chest. She looks up to him.

"Baby, you showed me something in that elevator. You said you would look after me, and you did. You made me feel so relaxed, that I did not have one panic attack. I believed you when you said you would protect me. I can't believe I am so relaxed in your arms." Dawn states. "You know how the refrigerator made me feel trapped? Well now I have the elevator, which makes me feel secure."

She kisses his lips, but it is more like a peck. Dean is surprised.

"What was that?" Dean asks.

"It just feels right. That was to show you and the world, that we're not intimate, but you're something special to me." Dawn states.

Dean is a little confused. He does not understand everything, but he is willing to accept it, if it allows him to get pecks on the lips. If she was any other lady, he would have forgotten about her. He would have bragged to Jason later that she was a head case, and not worth the drama. But this is Dawn, the love of his life.

"Are you a good friend? I hope you don't try to use me like pretty girls do men." Dean jokes more because he does not know what else to say. I mean the girl you love pecks you on the lips, but states that she is just a friend. That will play with any man's emotions.

Dawn does not laugh at his joke. "No, I'm not like that. In fact, I want to help you with a problem of yours. There is an empty apartment across from me. I want to speak to the owner on your behalf. The rent is good, and the area is even better. Would you like that?" Dawn asks.

"I would love that." Dean replies.

"You will like being closer to work?" Dawn asks.

"I will like being closer to you." Dean answers.

They finish eating, and they take a cab to Dawn's apartment. The cab ride takes about twenty minutes. The plan is for Dean to see Dawn in safely, and then take the cab home.

"Thanks for walking me in." Dawn states, and then thinks for a while. "You can't go all the way to Brooklyn at this time, and the cab ride will cost you. Come on inside. I can fix a place for you on the couch."

"Ok, but no hanky panky." Dean jokes.

"Hanky-panky? You're such a corn-ball." Dawn teases. She laughs at her own joke, as she opens the door to her apartment. Before she goes in, she points to the apartment across the hall, which is empty. "That is the empty apartment. Too bad you can't see it, but it is similar to mine."

Dawn's apartment is neat and nicely furnished. It is a colorful apartment, and nicely decorated. Dean looks at the couch.

"This couch is too small for me. I'm going home." Dean states.

"No, don't go. I will sleep on the couch and you can have the bed." Dawn states.

"I can't put you out like that. Look, we can both share the bed. If we are friends, then you can trust me." Dean states with sincerity.

"Can I trust you to behave?" Dawn asks with a smile.

"I promise I won't try a thing. I need a shower." Dean states as he pulls on his shirt like it is sticking to him. He is also slightly sweating because it is a humid night.

Dawn gives him a towel and a wash cloth, and then shows him to the bathroom. As he is taking his shower, Dawn is getting her things ready for her shower. She then sits, and thinks is she doing the right thing by letting him sleep in her apartment. She dismisses thoughts of him being a killer or a rapist. She convinces herself that she trusts him. He is sincere in his love for her, and is her protector. She justifies how she is a good judge of character, and how Dean can't be faking his love for her. She also reminds herself of how comfortably she slept in his arms, how good he felt, and how she is sure she is doing the right thing. She would bet her life on it, and in fact, she is betting her life on it. She can not believe this is someone she just met. She feels like she has known him for years.

Dean comes out of the bathroom with a towel over his lower body. He walks into the bedroom, where Dawn is. Dawn is about to go into the shower, when she looks at his towel.

"You can take off your towel, you have underwear on right?" Dawn asks.

"Yeah, but I'm shy." Dean answers.

"You were not that shy about me taking my bra off earlier." Dawn argues.

Dawn pulls the towel off of Dean who tries to hold it on. He has on red underwear, as Dawn laughs at him.

"Oh, we have a freak of the week up in here. Red underwear huh?" Dawn jokes as she goes to the shower.

"We'll see what is what when you come out with another granny bra." Dean yells behind her.

Dean sits on the bed. He looks around the room, and sees a dresser. He wonders about what kind of underwear she wears, but rules out going through her drawers. He is busy wondering what his chances of doing something with Dawn are, but rules that out as well. He reasons that he already promised not to try anything, and should not ruin it by trying something. If she tries something, then he would jump at the opportunity. Then he is ashamed at himself for thinking such things. He thinks this is not a hoe he met at the club, but the lady of his dreams. He is going to take this one slowly and carefully. It is strange how she pecked him on the lips. It is like giving him a taste of what he could not have. He loves the way she laid on him. She seems so comfortable around him, but he wonders what that was about. In the past, if a lady laid on him like that, he knew she was down for whatever; however, he had gotten close to Dawn because of a crisis, and the rules have changed. Maybe she is feeling close to him like a protective brother or something. Yeah he would have to play this carefully, especially since she has a potential boyfriend.

Dawn comes out of the shower in a robe. She opens the top of it to show Dean her new bra.

"Does this look like a granny's bra?" Dawn states.

The bra is neon color, and looks like it is from Victoria Secrets. Dean looks and shakes his head.

"Now you see. Showing me that is like taking a fat hungry child to a candy store, and telling him not to eat anything. It's like turning on the furnace, and your not cold." Dean states.

Dawn laughs, "Girl you're crazy."

"Hold up. Wait one minute. You're not turning me into one of your girlfriends. Oookaay." Dean states.

Dawn thinks back to what she stated, and starts laughing. 'I called you girl because I feel comfortable with you. I didn't mean anything by it." Dawn laughs. "You may have a little sugar in your tank,

OOOOKKKKAAAYY." She states as she snaps her fingers twice. "We should get some rest."

"Yeah, neither of us will be going to work tomorrow. It's almost morning." Dean states.

They both lay down in bed. They each lie on their side of the bed.

In the morning, Dean wakes up, and Dawn is lying on his stomach again. She looks so comfortable, that he does not wake her. He puts his arm around her, and goes back to sleep. When he wakes up again, it is early afternoon. Dawn is not in bed. He gets up, and puts on his pants. He sees Dawn in the kitchen, making breakfast.

"Look at you cooking." Dean states, as you can hear the bacon popping. Dawn takes it out of the hot grease and places it on a napkin. The napkin draws the grease out of the bacon.

"I slept so well. You make a comfortable pillow. You also impress me with your integrity." Dawn states as she is scrambling some eggs.

"What do you mean?' Dean asks.

"Not many men can sleep next to this, and not try anything, although I felt this strange lump that kept moving." Dawn says.

"It stopped after I got the image of you, in the bra, out of my head." Dean states with a smile. He sits at the table, and looks at the time. It is 11:30 AM. He figures he did not call in for work, but imagines that they realized there was a blackout yesterday. His attention is on Dawn. She looks so cute, but is still doing her thing in the kitchen.

Dawn places a plate of food before him. She reaches over and pecks him on the lips. Dean looks puzzled, but Dawn carries on like nothing is wrong.

"Today we can see the owner about your apartment, and just spend the day together. " Dawn states.

"Hold up. What was that?" Dean asks.

"What?" Dawn asks.

"The kiss on the lips again."

"That was a friendship kiss. I am a very touchy feely person, and we talked about this in the restaurant." Dawn states.

"I heard of a kiss on the cheek, but not the lips?" Dean asks.

"Hey if you can't handle it, I won't do it. It's just that you do have soft lips "Friends don't kiss on the lips." Dean states.

"Like I said, I will stop it if it is too much for you." Dawn says.

"No, I'm just asking to try to understand it. I don't want it to stop." Dean states, not wanting to stop a good thing. "So what else do you do with friends?" Dean asks with a sneaky smile on his face. "Any tongue kissing or pole dancing?"

Dawn throws a pot holder at Dean, who ducks.

"Hey, I just want to know."

CHAPTER SIX:
THE DOUBLE DATE

It is a nice, calm, and airy night, which is a good night for a double date. Daren, Tonka, Jennifer, and Carmen, are out eating dinner at a nice restaurant. Everyone is dressed nicely, and all seems like they are having a good time. Everyone is talking and laughing.

"Would you like my bread Tonka?" Carmen asks.

Tonka takes the bread. "Thank you Carmen, you're so perfect." Tonka states as she smiles at him. Daren and Jennifer look on. They are smiling because they can't believe how well Tonka and Carmen are getting along. Carmen snuck into Tonka's good graces by continually offering him food. It seems to be working.

Carmen was nervous when Tonka first came over, but he complimented her on her nice she looks. This gave Carmen enough confidence to talk to him. Jennifer and Daren are amazed at how uneasy Carmen is around Tonka. They are use to her bossing her men around, but she seems different with Tonka.

"I want to dance Daren." Jennifer states as she grabs Daren's arm. She really wants to give Tonka and Carmen some private time.

"So go ahead." Daren says jokingly.

"Daren." Jennifer whines.

"Just joking." Daren says as he gets up and walks with Jennifer to the dance floor. They start dancing to a slow song.

"They sure are hitting it off. All Carmen did all night was offered him food. He's going to love her by the end of the evening." Dean states. "I have never see Carmen act so loving. She is in love. Did you see the way her eyes light up when she looks at him?"

"Carmen is in love. She also has a gift when it comes to getting the man she wants. I have never seen Tonka take to anyone like that. Have you?" Jennifer states proudly of her friend.

"No I have not. She is in there, as long as she doesn't eat out of his plate."

"She said she is going to try to eat out of his plate." Jennifer states calmly.

"What! We all talked about this, and I told her no." Daren states alarmed.

"She said that will be the true test of love, if he lets her eat from his plate." Jennifer states.

"I have known Tonka all of his life, and I can't eat from his plate. Hell, his mother doesn't even eat from his plate. I told you that."

"She is good. She knows what she is doing." Jennifer states.

Daren leaves the dance floor with concern.

"We have to stop her. You have to tell her not to." Daren says with concern.

Just then a loud scream is heard from where Tonka and Carmen are. Daren and Jennifer stop short. They both look at each other and say, "Ouch!" at the same time, as they screw up their faces.

Later, Carmen is sitting down wondering how she got to this point. Something many people, where she is, would often wonder. Her sitting down gives her time to reflect. She does not think about the pain she feels because her heart is hurting more. She can not blame him, she has miscalculated. Like a swimmer who goes into the great white's turf, can't blame the shark, when he is bitten. It is her who rushed things, which is a mistake she will not make again. She sits there being wheeled into the hospital emergency room. Her legs are still working, so she does not understand why she is being wheeled into the emergency room. She can see Jennifer by her side telling her it will be OK, and Daren is wheeling her into the emergency room. She can hear Tonka trying to explain to Daren why Carmen has a fork in her right hand.

"It is not my fault; it is a reflex." Tonka stated.

Next, Carmen wakes up from her sleep. She would have thought the night a dream, but there was Jennifer sitting in a chair.

"How do you feel?" Jennifer asks.

"Sleepy. They put me to sleep?"

"No, you fell asleep because of the strong pain killer they gave you." Jennifer answers.

Carmen looks at her right hand. She sees that she has stitches, and Jennifer sees her looking.

"Your hand is fine, other than the puncture wounds. They gave you some anti biotic."

"I can't believe I underestimated him." Carmen states.

"You can't win them all. I told you Tonka is different. You were doing so well though. Oh, he told me to tell you sorry." Jennifer states.

"You think this is over? He does not know who he is messing with." Carmen states with a determine look on her face.

"But he stuck a fork in your hand." Jennifer states, looking at Carmen in disbelief.

"I will have found my soul mate, if I can get him to love me like he loves his food. I'm not giving up my happiness that easily. Don't you think I have the right to be happy?"

"But he stuck a fork in your hand." Jennifer repeats trying to make her get it.

"I heard you the first time." Carmen states to silence Jennifer. "Think about it. He loves his food, protects his food, nurtures it, and most of all eats it." Carmen smiles. "What women would not want to be treated like that?"

"He is treating you like his food. He stuck a fork in you." Jennifer states.

"He will be mine. This little pain was my mistake, not his. I jumped the gun on the relationship, but I almost had him. You saw it, he was all mines." Carmen states.

"But he stuck a fork in your hand." Jennifer repeats.
Carmen looks at her. "You're getting on my nerves. Can't you see I'm in love? I swear if I can't have him, then I will never love again."

"So what's your next move?" Jennifer asks.

"I figure, the way to his heart is through his stomach. That's how the saying goes. I'm going to cook for him every night of the week."

Carmen is uses to getting her way for selfish reasons, so why shouldn't she have her way for love. She will win his heart and will not take no for an answer, but love takes two people, doesn't it?

CHAPTER SEVEN:
OPERATION FEED

Carmen is seen putting all kinds of food before Tonka. One night it is steak and potatoes. Another night it is chicken, rice, and vegetable. Another night it is lasagna. Another night it is fried pork chops with mash potatoes. Carmen feeds him every night of the week, but Tonka still has not tried to make a move on her. She is perplexed. That Friday night, after dinner, she calls Tonka over to the couch, but he sits on the other side of the couch.

"Why don't you sit over here with me?" Carmen states as she is patting the spot she wants him to sit in.

"I'm good over here." Tonka says as he looks around.

Carmen pulls out a miniature candy bar. Tonka sees it and comes over to her. He eats the candy bar, and she puts her hand around him. She reaches over to kiss him, but the microwave bell sounds, and he jumps up.

"Popcorn, Yum." Tonka states as he runs into the kitchen.

Carmen has a look of frustration on her face.

The next day Carmen goes to vent at Jennifer's home. Carmen enters the apartment, and sits on her favorite spot on the couch. Jennifer can tell something is wrong, so she sits down and waits for Carmen to start.

"I am at my end. I have fed him for a week, and he has not tried to kiss me once. I don't know what I'm doing wrong. He likes food, I give him food, so what's the problem." Carmen complains.

"You don't get it. If he was to fall in love with the person giving him food, he would love the waitresses who bring him food. He is not associating the food with you. You need to get on his plate with the food." Jennifer jokes.

Carmen is about to say something smart to Jennifer, but then she thinks for a few seconds. Jennifer sees her, and states, "I was just joking about getting on his plate."

Carmen ignores her because she is still thinking.

"You---" Jennifer starts to say, but is cut off.

"Shush." Carmen states as she is still thinking. Carmen is looking up in the air, still deep in thought.

"Don't shush me—"

"Shush." Carmen states again. Jennifer looks at her with disgust.

"You gave me an idea. I'm not done yet."

"What now?" Jennifer asks

"I will give him a gift that will associate the food with me. I will give him a plate with my picture on it. That way, every time he eats, which is often, he will see me." Carmen answers.

"He will see you alright, but only after the food is gone. He will associate you with his food being gone, and that is not a good thing."

"No he will be full by the food, and will associate me with that satisfying feeling." Carmen explains.

"So you will invite him over every night again?" Jennifer asks

"No. In fact, I'm going to leave him alone for a week. If I am right, he will call me." Carmen explains.

CHAPTER EIGHT: DEAN'S APARTMENT

Over the past few weeks, Dean was able to rent the apartment across from Dawn's apartment. He previous landlord gave him another week extension, after he talked with Dawn. Dawn talked to him in person, and he cooperated with her. The new landlord accepted the reference Dawn gave him, and did not mind he could not get a reference from his previous landlord. Dean explained the problem he had at his previous residence, and the landlord understood.

Dean paid movers to move his things in, a few days ago. Now he is putting things in order, as well as buying some news things. He put up some nice paintings. One in particular is a painting of African American Sheriffs of the old West. He likes the way they held their guns out, and the proud look on their faces. He does not know exactly why it makes him feel so proud, but he paid the seven hundred dollars the artist asked for it. He put it on the wall across from the main coach, and just above the new big screen TV. His apartment is otherwise basic. He had a nice carpet laid down, and a comfortable couch, which is where he knows he will spend most of his time. He has a radio system on an entertainment set, the TV. sits on. The speakers and the surround sound used the same amp. Watching TV. or DVD. will feel like a movie experience. He brought the new TV. anticipating many nights watching TV with Dawn.

Dawn opens the front door and comes in. Dean watches her not only admiring her beauty, but loving the fact that she just walks right in.

"Look at this. You're all set, and so quickly. "Dawn states, looking around.

"I could not have done it without you getting me the apartment." Dean states.

"It was nothing. Hey, I'm coming over tonight to watch TV." Dawn states, looking at the TV. system. This is just what Dean had hoped she would say.

Dawn comes over and pecks him on the lips. She then sits on the couch.

"This is comfortable." Dawn states as she makes herself comfortable.

Dean, who is already sitting down, asks, "What are we watching?"

"It's a horror movie. You like horror?" Dawn asks.

"Not really, but as long as you are there to protect me, I'll be OK." Dean jokes.

"I'll go home and change into something comfortable, and will be right back in about an hour." Dawn answers as she leaves the apartment.

An hour later, Dean is watching TV. He looks at the door, and then back at the TV. He gets up, goes outside, and knocks on Dawn's door. There is no answer. He listens to the door, but hears nothing. He then returns to his apartment looking puzzled. He once again is watching TV. and falls asleep. There is a knock on the door. Dean takes his time getting up because he is half asleep. He opens the door, and it is Dawn. She is dressed up.

"Well, well, look who it is." Dean says sarcastically. He knows by her dress that she went out.

Sensing the sarcasm, Dawn instantly starts apologizing. "Sorry. Barry showed up, and took me out to eat." She remains in the doorway because Dean is not letting her in.

"You could have told me something. I hate to be kept waiting." Dean states.

"Sorry I forgot. I just got distracted when he showed up." Dawn explains.

"Well Hurrah for you."

She walks over to him and hugs him. She knows what she did was wrong, but Barry showed up, and she was not thinking straight. Now she needs to make it right with her friend.

"I'm sorry, but I had the most wonderful time." She states as she tries to enter the apartment. Dean is still in her way. She looks into his eyes, and he melts. He moves out of her way as she enters, and sits on the couch. She appears tired, as Dean sits down near her.

"I truly am sorry. I was so shocked he called that I forgot about everything else. Don't trip on me now. Remember I need you." Dawn states as she lies on his stomach.

"Just know I don't want to be treated like dirt by no one." Dean explains. "And you owe me a scary movie."

"Tomorrow, I promise." Dawn states.

"Your promises don't mean much."

"Nothing but death will keep me from it." Dawn jokes like the scene from the Color Purple.

Dawn and Dean start patting hands and singing. "You and I must never part, my keyama." They both start laughing.

"Ok, I have to go to work tomorrow and I am tired." Dean states.

Dawn is lying comfortably on his chest. "Just give me a few more minutes. I feel so comfortable." She says as she moves a little to his right.

"You should have seen him tonight. It was like every one wanted to be next to him, but I was the one next to him. When we danced, it was like we were floating on air. I'm sorry is this bothering you?"

"No, because you will be my girl, and there is no way you are going to fall for Barry." Dean states.

"Why not?" Dawn asks.

"He is a young football star. You think he is going to be faithful to you?" Dean asks.

"He will."

"You have a lot to learn about men." Dean replies.

"I believe in him."

"You see his face and his fame, and that is what makes you so tingly inside, but I know you. You will see the real him in time. You are mine, and no one knows you like me." Dean states.

Dawn looks into his eyes. "I'm amazed at how sure of that you are, but I do not feel anything for you except friendship. Even if I did fall in love with you, I would not mess with our friendship. I feel so close to you, and have not even known you that long." Dawn gets up.

"I'm amazed. Those are your favorite words." Dean jokes.

"I'm amazed you noticed that. I'm amazed you came up with that all on your own. I'm amazed--"

"Alright already." Dean states as he looks at her.

"That Black dress looks so good on you." Dean states.

"Thank you." Dawn says as her eyes light up with joy. She gets up and starts for the door.

"Well, I better get going." Dawn states.

"You like it when I flirt with you." Dean states.

"I don't like it, I love it." Dawn states. "It feels so good to have someone so in love with you. You know what I mean?"

Dean looks at her with a sad face. "No."

"Tomorrow?" Dean asks trying to lighten up the moment.

"You know it." Dawn answers. Dean goes to close the door. Dawn stops him.

"Where is my kiss?" Dawn asks. They peck each other on the lips, but Dawn holds on a little longer this time. She pulls away slowly, and leaves one hand around his neck, for a few seconds. She then walks towards her apartment, and opens the door. Dean watches her walk into her apartment.

Dawn stops. "I can feel your eyes on my butt." Dawn states.

"Ah hell, I'm looking, and what?"

Dawn perks her butt up more, and starts teasing Dean. Dean runs after her, but she makes it in her apartment, before he reaches her. Dawn is heard laughing on the other side of the door.

CHAPTER NINE:
THREE IS A CROWD?

Dean is sitting in his apartment when he hears a knock on the door. He takes his time answering, not wanting to appear eager, but in reality, he has been waiting for this all day.

"Come in." Dean says calmly. Dawn and her female friend, Cheryl, enter. Dawn's friend has Dawn's nice shape, which often makes men think that those types of female walk in groups. Their bodies are identical, but Cheryl is lighter then Dawn. She also could not compare to Dawn's beauty, but then again, few ladies could. Cheryl is a beauty in her own right. She gets her share of attention from men, but recently decided to calm it down a bit.

One night, she met this guy at a club, one thing led to another, and she found herself the victim of a one night stand. She never meant for it to happen, but he kissed so well, and got her so hot. She did not want to go to his place or take him to hers, so they did it in a hotel. She did not like the way she felt afterwards. He called her the next day, but she did not want to see him again. She did not want to be reminded of her cheap thrill. Her mother had always told her that her pussy is a gift. It is not a card gift that you give to everyone, but a solid gold gift meant for that special person. She usually made men wait around a month or two depending on the person. Now she vowed only to give it to that special person. It's not enough for her to want to do it, but the guy has to deserve it.

Dawn and Cheryl met at work, but Dawn no longer works at the advertisement firm Dawn still works at. Cheryl used to be Dawn's secretary. They became good friends, as they spent many late nights working on how to sell a certain product in the market. They bonded as they talked about each other's personal life. It was Dawn who encouraged Cheryl to go back to school, and she did. She was not able to get a job at the advertising company, but found one in another company. She kept in touch with Dawn for years, and they would hang out every now and then. They talk on the phone at least twice a week.

"Dean, I want you to meet my friend Cheryl." Dawn states.

"Hi Cheryl." Dean says as he approaches her. Cheryl holds her hand out, and Dean shakes it. She has a firm hand shake, which she may have learned from being in a male dominated business world.

"Hi, nice to meet you." Cheryl states with a friendly smile, which contradicts her hand shake. Their greeting is further contrasts, as Dawn gives Dean a peck on the lips.

"We still are watching the movie?" Dean asks Dawn because he is a puzzled why she brought a friend.

"Yeah, can Cheryl watch with us?" Dawn asks.

"Of course." Dean states, "But she has to get butt naked like you do."

Cheryl looks at him like he is crazy.

"Shut up silly." Dawn states and she looks at Dean and laughs. She looks at Cheryl. "You have to excuse my friend."

Cheryl smiles at them both.

An hour later, the three are on the couch, watching a movie, and eating popcorn. Dawn is sitting in the middle. Dawn taps Cheryl, and then says to Dean. "You see, he deserved to die because all men are dogs."

Dawn and Cheryl laugh and look at Dean. Dean looks at them, and starts barking. He gets close to Dawn's face and starts smelling her. Dawn and Cheryl start laughing. Dawn tries to stop Dean, but he continues.

"Stop!" Dawn states, but Dean continues by licking her face.

Dawn takes one of her chips, and holds it up. "Here boy. Want some chips, boy?"

Dean peps up, and sticks out his tongue like a dog would. Dawn holds it to Dean's mouth and Dean almost bites off her hand. The ladies start laughing. Dean eats the chip, and then goes close to Dawn, and starts licking her face again. Dawn tries to push him away, as she is laughing.

"Stop Dean---yuk. Ok, men are not dogs" Dawn states.

Cheryl looks at them as Dean stops

"You two are crazy." Cheryl states as she looks at them. They settle down and start watching TV. again.

"You see, this is why I can't marry an actress." Dean states as he points at the TV. "Look at this sex scene. He is all over her. Touching her butt and breast, damn."

"It's just acting." Dawn states, as Cheryl looks on.

"Acting my ass. No one is going to touch my wife like that." Dean says. "No wonder marriage between actors, don't last."

"I agree with Dawn, they are just acting." Cheryl states.

"Ok. Then let me touch you ladies up, and I will pay you." Dean states.

"You pay me 10-20 million, and you can squeeze my ass." Dawn replies as she laughs with Cheryl, who agrees with her.

"I'll owe you." Dean answers as he goes to grab Dawn's buttocks.

"Try it and you're dead." Dawn puts up her fist and looks at him. She starts smiling because she knows he is joking.

"They have to have sex scenes in movies; if not, how do they do the sex scenes."

"They can be implied. You see two people go into the bedroom, and they come out putting on their clothing." Dean says.

"That won't work. People want to see it." Dawn answers.

"Only perverts want to see. They get their jollies off of it." Dean states. "Some movies will throw a sex scene in a movie, when it is not needed."

"Look these actors get paid a lot, so they should take off something or allow something to be touched." Cheryl states.

"Well what makes them different than prostitutes, except for the high price money?" Dean asks. "I mean they get touched, allow millions of people to see them naked, and get paid for it."

"I see your point, it would destroy a marriage." Dawn states.

"I don't know" Cheryl states. "I still feel it's acting."

"So would you let your husband kiss on an actress, and simulate sex with her?" Dean asks.

"I don't know, because I am not in that situation. It's hard to say." Cheryl states.

"That is a no." Dawn says and laughs to Dean. Cheryl pushes Dawn.

After spending time watching TV. and joking, Dawn gets up from lying on Dean, and Cheryl gets off the couch. Cheryl and Dawn go to the door to leave, as Dawn pecks Dean on the lips. Dawn and Cheryl then leave Dean's apartment, and enter Dawn's apartment.

"What's going on here? I thought you were dating Barry?" Cheryl asks when they close the door.

"I am." Dawn answers.

"It seems like you two are dating because you were all over him." Cheryl states.

"No. He likes me, but we are just friends. He is nice too. He looked out for me when I was bugging out about being stuck in the elevator. He's a good guy." Dawn states.

"Yeah he seems cool." Cheryl answers as she is deep in thought with herself.

Meanwhile, at Tonka's apartment, Tonka is eating a late night snack. As he finishes, he looks at his plate, and sees a picture of Carmen with a wide eye smile. He stares at the empty plate, and smiles.

CHAPTER TEN:
THE CAB RIDE

Dean and Dawn are walking out of their apartment lobby together.

"You get the cab." Dean states.

"Why me?" Dawn asks.

"You had breakfast at my place, so you owe me, and they stop for you." Dean answers.

Dawn holds out her hand and a cab stops. They both get in.

"Did you enjoy last night?" Dawn asks.

"Yeah it was cool. Cheryl is cool too, but tonight I want you for myself." Dean states.

"I can't, I'm going out with Barry tonight. Sorry." Dawn answers. "What are you going to do tonight?"

"I don't know." Dean answers.

"You need a girl." Dawn states.

"I got a girl." Replies Dean as he looks at her, and kisses her on the cheek. She starts smiling.

"So, where are you going?" Dean asks.

"Out to eat again. I want you to meet him." Dawn states. Dean looks puzzled.

"Why?"

"You're my good friend and I want you to meet my man."

"Let him meet Cheryl." Dean states. He has no intention of meeting the man who has his girl.

"I want him to meet you."

"Once again, why?" Dean asks

"I want to see what you think of him."

"You know what I think of him." Dean answers.

"You don't know him."

"I know the type."

"You're wrong about this one." Dawn states.

"How long you knew Cheryl?" Dean asks wanting to change the subject.

"Long enough, Why?" Dawn asks, wondering why he is asking about her friend.

"She seems cool, I'm just asking." Dean states.

"That is the second time you brought her name up. You want her or something." Dawn asks.

"And if I did?" Dean asks and looks at Dawn smiling.

I'll leave that between you two." Dean sees that Dawn is acting a little jealous.

Dawn is quiet, and Dean is looking at her.

"You're the only one for me, you know that." Dean states.

"I don't know anything." Dawn states, not looking at him.

Dean takes her head, and turns it towards him. He looks deep in her eyes.

"You are." Dean reassures her. She smiles and leans on him.

Dean looks at the cab driver, who is an Arab man with a turban on his head, and a long beard. The cab drive has been looking back at them the entire ride. Dean notices it, and then starts smiling. Dawn looks at Dean and sees him smiling.

"Don't do it Dean, I know that look. Come on, not this morning."

Dean looks at her. "Why not this morning? You can sit here hugging me now, but all I can think about is how you slept with all of my friends." Dean states. He is talking loud enough for the cab driver to hear. The cab driver perks up, and starts looking at Dawn through the rear view mirror. Dawn has her head down and is shaking her head.

"You slept with John, David, Rahiem, and Born. I did not even mention my brother in the wheel chair."

The cab driver looks back at Dawn again. Dawn sees it.

"Mister he is lying." Dawn states, but the cab driver is still looking back at her and then at the road.

"Am I lying about the crabs you gave me? Am I lying about that too." Dean states as he starts scratching his private area. "You're getting these crabs all over this nice man's cab."

The cab driver looks uncomfortable. He starts brushing off his shoulder, and scratching his chest. Dawn looks at Dean and shakes her head. The cab stops as Dean jumps out of it. Dawn gives the man the money.

"Just drop it on the seat Ms." The cab driver states. Dawn drops the money on the seat and laughs to herself. She gets out of the cab, and looks at Dean.

"I'm going to kill you." She states.

That was just the start of her troubles with Dean in the cab. The worse was when she put her head down in Dean's lap, to rest. Dean saw it was the same cab driver, and he started closing his eyes, and twisting his face funny. Dawn did not see him because she had her eyes close. Dean act like Dawn is giving him a blow job. The cab driver was looking back so much, that he almost hit the car in front of him, on two separate incidents.

The next morning, Dean and Dawn had about five cabs waiting to take them to work.

CHAPTER ELEVEN:

SEX: THE GOOD: THE BAD, AND THE OH! OH! I'M CUMMING.

Carmen and Jennifer are talking, at Jennifer's home.

"Just like that he called me. I told you it would work." Carmen states with pride.

"He said he missed you, and wants to see you tonight. That is great. The picture plate worked." Jennifer states with admiration at Carmen's cleverness.

"Tonight, can you imagine? I'm going to rock his world." Carmen states with a look of passion in her eyes. Men have no problem loving her, but sex with her is like striking gold. Usually the men would cum quick because they can't believe they are making love with someone so beautiful. Carmen has given a few lucky men the honor of being pleasuring her, but they are too few and long in between. This is the first time she felt nervous about having sex with someone. Tonka made sparks fly inside of her, and she didn't really know why. All she knows is he is coming to her place, and she is going to use all her powers to get him in bed.

"Don't eat from his plate." Jennifer warns her. Carmen gently rubs the hand that was pierced with the fork.

"Naw, I'm taking my time with that. Tonight my man is going to eat from my plate." Carmen states, referring to her vagina.

"What are you going to do?" Jennifer asks.

"Whatever he will let me get away with. I got to go and get everything ready."

"How are you going to get him to the bedroom? Tonka thinks with his stomach, not the other thing men usually use." Jennifer states.

"I got it all planned out. I'm telling you, this is the one." Carmen states.

They hear a key entering the front door, as the door opens.

"That is Daren." Jennifer states.

"I'm on my way out." Carmen replies.

Carmen leaves as Daren comes in.

"Hi Daren. Bye Daren." Carmen states.

"Hey." Daren states as Carmen passes by. "Be good to my friend Tonka, you man eater."

"Shut up." Carmen answers.

Daren enters and kisses Jennifer. She looks at him, and he looks back at her.

"How was your day?" Jennifer asks.

"It was OK. These cases are getting to be too much." Daren replies.

"Being a social worker can be a hard job." Jennifer states as she goes behind him to rub his shoulders.

"How was your day?" Daren asks as he is puzzled as to why she is rubbing his shoulders.

"It was good. Some of us teachers want to get together with our boyfriends/husbands." Jennifer states.

"Oh yeah, good----Wait." Daren states.

"It's tomorrow, and it will be brief." Jennifer stops rubbing his shoulder, and comes around to explain.

"Oh no. I am not going." Daren states.

"Why not?" Jennifer asks, knowing the answer to her own question.

"Five of you will plan to go out with their man, but only I will show up, and be stuck there with you and your friends. You all will talk to each other, and I will be there alone and bored." Daren states. He knows the routine because it has happened before to him.

"We all promised to bring our mates to the dinner. I don't want to be the only one there without my mate." Jennifer explains.

"No way."

"I'll make a deal with you. You can leave if you are the only man there." Jennifer states.

"No because I know you. You will not let me leave." Daren protests.

"Come on baby. I'd do it for you."

"I wouldn't ask you to do it for me." Daren stated.

"Please." Jennifer begs.

"Ok, but if I am the only one there, I'm going to get you." Daren states.

Jennifer is so happy that she kisses him on the lips. She always has been able to get her way with Daren, and is one of the few people who could.

Later that night, Carmen is on the couch with Tonka. Her home is filled with scented candles. Her wardrobe is very revealing. From her low cut blouse, to her short cut skirt. It is a little to revealing for her taste. She has always got her man by looking classy. Tonka had her doing things she would not normally do. For example, she is an excellent cook, but has never thought enough of her previous associates to cook for them. For Tonka, she has cooked at least seven meals. This is not including her meal for him tonight. She knows Tonka is not interested in her classy clothing, but she knows he sees what he likes and takes it. He has done that with his food, and she hopes with her. She shows him a little flesh hoping he will like what he sees. So far, he has hardly noticed her low cut blouse or her tight skirt. Here they are, on the couch again, Tonka on one end, Carmen on the other end, and Carmen is out of moves.

"So did you enjoy dinner?" Carmen asks trying to buy her time, and figure out what to do.

"Yeah." Tonka states.

"So what made you call?" Carmen asks.

"I don't know. I was just missing you. Your face is constantly on my mind. In fact, I can't get your face out of my mind." Tonka states.

"Well can I get a hug?" Carmen asks with a smile on her face. She has done fake smiles before, but this smile is sincere. Tonka had her feeling like a little school girl in love. She secretly loved that feeling, and they way Tonka made her feel inside. Yeah, her smile to him is sincere. It came from the butterflies in her stomach, and the goose bumps on her arms.

Tonka gets up of the couch, as Carmen stands up. Tonka gives her a big strong bear hug. Carmen closes her eyes to fully enjoy the hug. Tonka lets her go, but sits back on the other side of the couch. Carmen sits back down in her spot at the other side.

"That felt good. How come you never once tried to kiss me?" Carmen asks.

"I'm shy." Tonka states.

Carmen takes out some chocolate frosting, and puts it on her lips, as Tonka watches her. It is a back up plan she had to make Tonka kiss her.

"Can you wipe this off my lips?" She asks innocently.

Tonka charges her and starts kissing her. Carmen is surprise, but is enjoying it. Her legs are shaking, but then Tonka suddenly stops. Carmen comes up breathing heavy.

"That was incredible. Why did you stop?" Carmen asks.

"I got the chocolate off." Tonka replies.

Carmen gets an idea. She runs to the refrigerator, and then to her bedroom.

"Is everything OK." Tonka yells, looking at the bedroom door.

"Give me a minute, and then come in when I call you." Carmen states. "I have a treat for you."

She calls him in. She is lying on the bed, naked with two whip cream cans in her hands. Her private area and chest is covered with whip cream. Tonka looks at her and starts breathing heavily.

"I better go." Tonka states.

"Wait. You can go after you finish your desert." Carmen states.

Tonka eyes light up. "That is whip cream huh?" He asks.

"It's desert baby, so come and get it." Carmen states as she thinks to herself, "If this does not work, I'm going to look like a damn fool."

Tonka stares at her, and starts ranting like an animal. There is a small table in his way. He tosses the table, which flies across the room. He is getting ready to charge Carmen. Carmen looks at him, and is getting nervous.

"Wait, take it easy with me. Be gentle."

Tonka charges her, and starts eating her out. Carmen's nervous face turns to pleasure as she starts groaning. She starts screaming in joy. She is in extreme pleasure. She grabs the back board, which braces her body. Her head turns to the side, and she closes her eyes. Her body tightens up, and then releases slowly. She peeks, and then puts a slash mark on her head board. She sees Tonka is still going.

"I need to rest for a minute. I got mine." She states, but Tonka is still going at it. She tries to talk again, but she gets right back into it.

"Never mind, keep doing what you're doing baby." Carmen moans.

CHAPTER TWELVE:
LOVE, WHAT IS IT GOOD FOR? ABSOLUTELY NOTHING.

Dean is on his couch watching TV. It is a Saturday night. He should be out partying. Jason and he are old party animals. He thought about calling Jason, since he has not heard from him in a while, but decides to stay in and watch TV. Strange, he never thought he would be content just watching TV, but he is comfortable with that.

Suddenly he hears someone coming through the front door, and knows it is Dawn. It's Dawn with a gorgeous dress on. She is looking sad.

"I don't know what happened to him. He said he would pick me up at 8 PM. It is 11 PM. now." Dawn complain as she kisses Dean on the lips, and sits down in his lap. She seems to be acting like a baby, wanting Dean to cradle her. Dean hugs her, but looks a little uncomfortable.

"Maybe he was in an accident." Dean asks with a smile on his face, but Dawn misses the humor.

"No, I tried the nearest hospital already." Dawn states.

Dawn lies on his shoulder.

"I swear it hurts like hell." Dawn states, as she hugs Dean tighter.

"What?" Dean asks.

"Waiting on someone to show. I hate it because it reminds me of my father." Dawn states.

"Oh how you did me a few days ago." Dean says. He knows it is not the time to bring that up, but could not help himself.

"I said I was sorry." Dawn states as she lifts off of him, and looks in his face.

"I know. Come here." Dean pulls her back. She welcomes his hug.

Dawn stops for a second, and looks down at Dean's legs. She jumps out of his lap.

"You guys all have a one track mind. Sex, Sex, Sex." Dawn states as she stands up.

"It's involuntary. It's involuntary." Dean tries to explain.

"Dag, you almost rose me up in the air."

"Hey, you sat your fat ass right on it. I can't help that." Dean tries to explain.

"Can't you leave your feeling out of it for a second?" Dawn states while still standing.

"No, I can't. And what do you mean when you said you men?" Dean asks.

Dean thinks for a second, as Dawn looks away.

"I know you didn't." Dean states as he stands up and walks towards her.

"It's my fault. I opened too much of myself up to him. Now he does not want to deal with me." Dawn states.

"What are you saying?" Dean asks concerned.

"On our third date, which was our last date, he took me to his home." Dawn states as she looks down at the ground.

"No you didn't. You better not have." Dean warns.

"I did." Dawn says sheepishly.

"You had sex with Barry? A football player who has girls around him all the time." Dean yells as Dawn shakes her head yes. She looks like she is about to cry. Dean is pacing and looking at her.

"This friendship is not working." Dean states.

"What? Because I had sex with him? I care for him." Dawn states.

"And I care too much for you to know these things." Dean states.

"I need a friend Dean, not a lover."

"And I need a lover. Why does it always have to be your way?" Dean asks.

"If we do something, we will lose the friendship."

"And gain a better friendship, love." Dean states.

"I don't feel for you that way."

"So I must have you tease me, constantly seeing the food, but never able to taste it." Dean states.

Dawn starts crying and screaming. "So what are you saying, we can't be friends no more."

Dean says nothing.

"Dean get me out of that refrigerator. I need to be in the elevator with you." Dawn states.

Dean just sits on the couch with his head down. She thinks for a second, and goes over to the couch. She takes off her underwear, and lies down on the couch.

"We have to fuck to stay friends then come on. No good will come from it. Come on. You want what he had, come on." She screams.

"You think I won't." Dean states.

"I am offering it to you. Come on. Get this shit over with."

Dean jumps on her and starts kissing her, but she does not kiss him back. He touches her breast, but she is crying. He then gets off of her and sits on the couch.

"What's the matter? You cum already---." Dawn states sarcastically.

Dawn stops short. She sees his eyes, and sees that he is also crying. Dawn runs to him to hold him, and they both start crying.

"I have not cried since I was a little child, much less in front of anyone." Dean states.

"Why are you crying?" Dawn asks.

"Can't you see that I am hurting? You're my girl; you're not supposed to sleep with no one else." Dean explains.

"But I'm not your girl."

"You are, but just don't know it yet." Dean answers.

"I need this right now. To be in your arms like this is my peace. To kiss your lips is so innocent, and yet so tranquil." Dawn states.

"That is love." Dean states simply.

"No it is peace. I like having that with you."

"Well can you stop doing those things?" Dean asks.

"I depend upon those things."

"How come you can't get that peace from Barry?"

"That is lust. I get that tingling feeling when I see him." Dawn answers.

"We need to stop this cuddling, and kissing on the lips. It's sending my body mixed messages." Dean states.

"If you want to, but I don't want to. You are so cuddly. You still love me right?" Dawn asks.

"I love you, and you will be my girl one day. You will see that you do love me."

"I don't see it, but when I look into your eyes, you make it seem so true. It's getting late." Dawn states, as she gets up and walks to the door. She starts to peck him on the lips, but catches herself. She holds out her hand.

"That seems so formal. How about a kiss on the cheek?" Dean asks.

"Ok." Dawn replies, as she kisses his cheek, and then goes home.

After she leaves, Dean sits on the couch to replay the entire evening in his mind. He does not want her to stop laying on him, and kissing him on the lips, but said that out of the hurt that he felt. There was also some deep down hurt over her sleeping with Barry. He knew it would happen, but did not expect to hear about it so soon. He drinks a nice cup of tea to settle him, and then goes to bed.

Hours later, Dean is in bed sleeping. He hears a knock on the door. He gets up and walks to the door. He opens it, and it is Dawn in her pajamas.

"I can't sleep. I know I said I can do without, but I can't. I need my kiss, and my cuddle." Dawn states.

Dean walks back to the bedroom. Dawn closes the door and follows him. They both get into bed, and Dawn lays on his chest. She props herself up, and kisses his lips.

"Good night. I do love you. It is friendship love, but it is still love." Dawn says, but Dean does not answer her. She lies back down on his chest, and they fall asleep.

CHAPTER THIRTEEN:
BLISS

Carmen's bedroom is quiet, except for the steady humming of the fan. The sheets are all over the floor. Tonka is laying there in his underwear, but Carmen is not there. The head board has seven hash marks in it. A happy Carmen comes in the room with a tray of food. She says nothing, but the smell of the food smacks Tonka in the face. He wakes up to bacon, eggs, and grits.

"Good morning Tonka." Carmen calls.

Carmen sits down beside him, and starts feeding him. She is looking at him with admiration. Her body needs rest, but she just had to make breakfast for him. Her love for him made her do things she would not normally do, and she did them happily. She pats herself on the back for recognizing that he would be a great lover. The best she had ever had. A sadness falls over her as she realizes that she has his body, but still does not have his love.

Carmen starts talking to Tonka as she is feeding him. She is moving too slowly, so Tonka takes the fork from her.

"Last night was incredible. I never believed the body could endure such pleasures, or give such pleasures. Where have you been all my life? I want you here with me. I'm really feeling you baby. I knew since the first time I met you, that you are the one. So what do you say? Will you stay here with me?" Carmen asks. Tonka does not answer. She touches his shoulder and says, "Tonka?"

Tonka looks up from his food. "What? I didn't hear you."

"Never mind." Carmen answers in a plain voice.

CHAPTER FOURTEEN: THE MALL

Dean is waking up, and Dawn starts to get up as well.

"How did you sleep?" Dean asks.

She cuddles close to him. "Like a baby. You need to take your chest, bottle it, and sell it to those who can't sleep." Dawn states.

"What you doing today?" Dean asks her.

"Shopping, you coming?"

"I hate shopping." Dean answers with a frown on his face.

"Yeah, but you love me."

"Ask Cheryl to go with you."

"I want you to go. Cheryl is coming over to watch a movie tonight because she had so much fun before. You in?" Dawn asks.

"Yeah, I'm down." Dean replies.

"What about going shopping with me? It's more fun when you come with me. Plus men don't nag me as much when I have another man with me."

"Alright, I need some shirts anyway." Dean gives in to her.

Dean and Dawn are at the shopping mall. They both have bags in their hands. Dean goes inside the men's bathroom, as Dawn waits outside for him. Two men approach her. One is dressed in a blue jean outfit. He has on a tan shirt that matches his tan timberland boots. He has a large gold medallion. Despite the heat, he chose to wear the outfit any way. To follow suit, his friend has on a black jean outfit, with some burgundy looking timberlands. They both would rather fry, then to not look fly.

"Dam you got a fat ass." Man one says as he approaches Dawn. She rolls her eyes and tries to walk away from the men.

"Where you going baby, my man wants a date with you?" Man two asks.

"I'm not interested, so keep it moving." Dawn replies.

"We did not ask are you interested. We're just window shopping." Man Two states as he gives Man one a pound.

"Yeah and I see something I want, but the question is how much?" Man one asks.

"You two clowns had better keep walking before my boyfriend gets back." Dawn states angrily.

Man one puts his hand in her hair. Dawn moves his hand away from her.

"Get your nasty hand out of my hair. My man is gonna." Dawn states, but is cut off.

"Your man is gonna what? I don't see anyone." Man two argues.

Dean comes from out of nowhere and punches man one in the face. He then punches Man two in the stomach, and then in the face. Both men are down, as he starts kicking them both.

"Too bad your mother or Father never taught you to respect your black Queen." Dean yells. Dawn tries to stop him, but he keeps at it. She finally pulls him away, and grabs the bags. The men are on the ground moaning, as Dawn leads him into a restaurant. She takes a napkin, and starts wiping the sweat off of his face.

"What was that about? I could have handled them. Men approach me all the time." Dawn states.

"But they were being disrespectful. One was putting his hand in your hair, and the other was talking to you nasty."

"You're too jealous. When I'm out with other men guys approach me, and they don't fight like that." Dawn states.

"I am not other men or your precious Barry. Neither am I a fighter. If those men were teasing me, I would have ignored them." Dean states.

"You could have been killed."

Dean looks her directly in the eyes. "Look at me. You need to know that I am a man that will fight for your honor. I would die before I see harm come your way." Dean states.

"But----" Dawn starts to say, but is cut off.

"Do you understand that? It is important that you believe that." Dean states firmly.

Dawn looks into his eyes, and starts smiling.

"My own knight in shinning armor." Dawn says.

"Every princess should have one." Dean answers.

She knows she would never forgive herself if Dean had gotten hurt, but she likes the fact that Dean stood up for her. She loves the fact that he is willing to risk his life to protect her. After all, that is what women want. They want protection and security from their man. If a woman knows you are willing to die for them, and that you will not cheat on them, then they will be with you forever. Men on the other hand, just want to be respected.

They hop in a cab and return home. Dean enters his apartment, but turns back to Dawn. Dawn's voice is heard calling over to him.

"I'll be over after I put this away and take a shower." Dawn replies.

"Ok."

Dean put his bags in his bedroom. He will put them away later. He takes his shower, and makes something to eat. He saves a plate for Dawn, which is what he usually does on the weekends.

CHAPTER FIFTEEN:
OPPS, SHE DID IT AGAIN

A couple of hours later, Dean is sitting on the couch, watching TV, and dosing off. A knock is heard at the door.

"Where have you been? You're an hour late, and since when do you knock." He starts yelling at the door before he opens it. He opens the door and sees Cheryl.

"Oh hi. I thought you were Dawn." Dean explains.

"Hi, Dawn isn't here I take it?" Cheryl asks.

"No, she's not next door?" Dean asks.

"No, I was knocking for a while, and she didn't answer."

"We've been stood up again." Dean replies.

"Barry, right. I don't know what she sees in him. You treat her better then he does." Cheryl states.

"Oohhh, well come right in my dear. I like the way you talk." Dean laughs as Cheryl smiles and enters.

"No, I should be going." Cheryl says.

"Nonsense, we can still watch the movie. I even cooked. I hope you like ribs." Dean answers.

Cheryl is eating diner, as Dean and her watch TV. They both are at the dining room table.

"These ribs are off the hook. I don't know what people have against pork." Cheryl states.

"Yeah the pig gets a bad rap." Dean adds as they both laugh.

"They say the pig is a nasty animal. They seem clean to me." Cheryl argues.

"Some of my best friends are pigs." Dean jokes, as they both laugh.

"When you consider vegetables are grown in cow feces, which is nastiest?" Cheryl continues.

"I don't like vegetables, except for spinach."

"You want to be like Popeye huh?" Cheryl jokes, as she laughs like Popeye.

"Naw, I hated spinach when I was young, but now I love it. Go figure." Dean states.

"Look at the goat. It will eat paper, cans, or just about anything. You never hear people calling the goat nasty." Cheryl states.

"Yes, the pig is a persecuted animal."

"I know. We have to help it."

There is a pause, and then they both laugh.

"So how did you meet Dawn." Dean asks.

"We used to work together. We have been buddies every since." Cheryl states.

"You know I love her." Dean states firmly.

"She told me she loves Barry. Love is a bummer." Cheryl answers.

"So who are you dating?" Dean asks.

"No one right now because I am very much into my career. Plus all these men want is booty." Cheryl states.

"Can you blame them? The way these ladies are giving it up now a day." Dean defends his fellow men.

"Yeah, but I'm looking for romance." Cheryl states.

"I am as well."

"Then why are you not out there looking?" Cheryl asks.

"I'm in love with Dawn. She just does not know it yet." Dean states.

"You think you can convince her to get rid of Barry?" Cheryl asks

"I don't know. Only time will tell." Dean answers.

"Maybe you need to look for someone else. There are a lot of fish in the sea." Cheryl states.

"But only one that swims in my pond." Dean states.

"I hear that. Let's watch something." Cheryl says.

Dean starts switching channels.

"Can we watch this? I have always wanted to see this movie." Cheryl asks.

Dean doesn't want to see this chick flick, but thought he should be polite.

Cheryl looks at Dean. "Can I have my pillow?"

"Oh. OK, go right ahead." Dean replies, as he lifts up his arm, and Cheryl lies on his stomach.

"Dawn is right. You are comfortable. I could fall asleep right here, right now. Dawn is crazy." Cheryl says.

"What?" Dean asks.

"She got a perfectly good man going to waste." Cheryl states as they both laugh.

"And I don't like to waste things." Cheryl states. Dean laughs, but Cheryl does not. Dean stops laughing. Cheryl is looking at TV. as Dean looks at her.

His eyes scan her nice breast, thin waist, and thick hips. He stops because he thinks she sees him looking. He thinks she is flirting with him. He could definitely see himself hitting that, but she is Dawn's friend.

Dawn states Dean and her are just friends, but she would not want him sleeping with her friend.

"Naw." He thinks. "It would be foolish to risk her love just for some pussy. Then again, it has been a long time. Naw it's not worth it." Dean's penis and his brain are having another argument. His penis argues that he should consider Cheryl's fat ass, at least for his sake. He also argues the vicinity of it. It is right, and he could have it right now. Those are the penis' usual argument, ones which have gotten Dean many a AIDS. test in his club days. The penis would argue, hey look at that fat ass. If you don't hit it, someone else will. He would argue that if he took time to go to the store and get a condom, then the girl might not want to do it when he got back. Then he would argue that he should not pull out because it feels so good. Dean never listens to that one. The last thing he wants is to get one of these chicken heads pregnant. His common sensed rushes into his head, at the same time the cum rushes out of his penis. He would think, what have I done. I could have AIDS. He could not believe how foolish he could be, but thirty minutes later, he is doing the same thing. His argument then is, if she has AIDS, then a second time won't hurt. Those were Dean extremely foolish years.

His mind usually lost the old battles, but lately is starting to win. His mind convinced him of romance, and to be more carefully sexually. It really started when he heard one of a friend of his who died from AIDS.

Meeting Dawn has also helped his mind to start winning. In fact, tonight is the first night the penis has tried to challenge him in a while, but he thinks about Dawn, and what she means to him, and the penis loses.

"I can't try anything." Dean thought, but like a good soldier, his penis stood at attention all night. "Yeah I lost this one." The penis would say to the brain. "But time is on my side, you can't hold out forever."

CHAPTER SIXTEEN: TRAINS AND PAINS

A man, with a transit vest, is in the train yard. He is getting into a box like compartment of a train. He is a small thin man, and is middle aged. He has many years working for transit, and is a supervisor. He has not let many Train operators fool him. He caught an Operator who lied about hitting a home signal (a term used to describe a red signal, which is illegally passed, by a train.) He proved the operator did it, and the operator was fired for lying. He knows Train operators do not like him, but all he cares about is getting promoted. He is squeezing his small frame in to the compartment, when another man with a transit vest, sees him.

"Fields, I thought I saw you get on this train. What are you doing?" Herman states.

"I am going to catch Train operator Tonka in the act." Fields states.

"What are you talking about?" Herman states. "You always have some scheme going."

"You know the Superintendent is upset because someone spilled hot sauce on the train control, and caused the entire panel to be sent for repairs. I know it had to be Tonka, and I'm going to catch him." Fields states.

"By hiding in the front compartment? You'll be a laughing stock if anyone finds out you went through all this to catch Tonka." Herman states.

Herman and Fields know that even his fellow supervisors would despise a man that would stoop that low. Everyone knows that Fields is looking to get promoted. Fields doesn't care what his co-workers think of him, but he knows the Superintendent would not give a promotion to a person who is hated by his co-workers. It would sow discord.

"I know, but if I prove it was him, the Superintendent will promote me for sure." Fields states.

"How are you going to catch him, if no one is to know you're hiding?" Herman asks.

"I have this camcorder that can film in the dark. I'm going to record him in the act through this hole." Fields states as he points to a hole in the compartment that is facing where the train operator sits.

"What if it's not him?" Herman asks.

"Oh it's him, and today he is going to be caught." Fields answers.

"You're crazy to go through all that just to catch someone." Herman states.

"Call me crazy today, but you will be calling me boss tomorrow." Fields answers.

About a half an hour later, Tonka is operating the Train, and comes to a stop. The Conductor is heard making announcements. He has a large brown paper bag next to him, which reads snack. He reaches into it, and pulls out a large pop pie. He sits it on the train console, and feels the top of it.

"Good it's still warm. Pork and bean pop pie, my favorite." Tonka states to himself.

Tonka starts to eat as Fields is in the compartment filming it. Field thinks he got him, and that promotion is in the bag. Tonka is pulling into another station, and taking the last of the Pork and bean pop pie. He throws it in the bag as garbage. He starts operating again, and a loud grumble is heard from his stomach. He moves a little, and has a puzzled look on his face. He moves a little more, and his stomach settles. He pulls into a station and a filthy looking, homeless woman, with dreads, knocks at his cab window.

"You da Train operator, dat put me friend in the hospital? He lost a lung cause you." Dread woman states in a heavy Jamaican accent.

"You don't want none lady, not today." Tonka states.

"Me know you fe one. I come all the way from the south side to get you." States. Dread woman, as she comes on the train and sits right by Tonka's cab door. Tonka comes out of his cab.

"Lady, you can't sit there." Tonka states.

"Ohh, can't take the smell, huh?" Dread woman states. "It gets worse den dis."

"Sit there and you will be sorry." Tonka tells her.

Tonka smells her, holds his nose, and runs back into the cab. Dread woman starts to fan her dirty dress. She opens her legs, and yells at the cab.

"I have me girlfriend, and me haven't washed in a week or so. Smell the burn." Dread woman states, as she laughs to herself.

Tonka pulls off out of the station. He smells the lady and starts to gag. Fields also smells Dread woman, and is holding his nose.

"What the hell." Fields states to himself.

The Dread woman is now taking off her socks, and revealing her smelly filthy feet. The people on the train run out of the subway car, looking like they are about to vomit. The Dread woman lifts up her underarms, and is yelling towards the cab.

"You see me no rump with you. You fe get dead, by the dread. You ready to give up. You better not pass out while driving the train. You see what happens if you fe test me." Dread woman states.

She starts laughing. Tonka is in the cab looking sick. He realizes that he has the window by him down, which pulls the bad air towards him. He puts his window up. This slows down the circulation of the air from Dread woman, to him.

"I got something for you. You want to play huh?" Tonka yells at the door to Dread woman.

Tonka opens the window on the other side of the cab. This causes the air to flow towards the opposite side of the cab, where Fields is hiding.

Tonka takes off again, and he can breathe again.

"Damn." Fields states as he covers his mouth, and is holding his nose. He puts down the camcorder. "What is that ungodly smell?"

Tonka stops at another station. He closes the window on the other side of him.

"Now we are heading for the tunnel. I will have you for a full three minutes, and you will have no where to run." Tonka states to himself, about Dread woman.

Tonka takes off again. He stands up, and is operating with one hand, as he starts dancing around. He starts passing gas as he is dancing.

"How you like me now?" Tonka states.

Dread woman smells the air, and her eyes start tearing. She covers her nose, and fights back the vomit.

"I'm not moving, and you will not beat me." She states to the cab door, which Tonka is behind.

Tonka is still dancing and passing gas.

"Owaht, Owaht." Tonka sung, as he passes gas two times to answer himself.

"Owaht, Owaht, Owaht." Tonka sung, as he answers back with three farts.

Dread Woman is about to pass out. She inhales and then vomits. She gets up to run away, but she passes out a few feet from her seat. Fields squint his eyes at the smell, and finally passes out. He falls out of the compartment and a shock Tonka jumps.

"What the? Supervisor Fields?" Tonka states. He stares at him for a few seconds, then turns back to the road. He sees a red light. He takes full breaks, and puts both hands on the train.

"Ahhhhhh! Stooooooppppppppp! Yoooooooddddddaaaaaaaa!" Tonka yells as he is concentrating. He is praying the train stops. The train stops just before the red signal, and he falls back into his seat.

Tonka leaves the train with Fields, as they get to the last stop.

"Listen, you don't tell anyone I was hiding in the compartment to catch you, and I won't tell the Superintendent you were eating on the console. What do you say? We have a deal?" Fields asks.

"Deal, but hiding like that is grimy." Tonka states.

"No, grimy is that ungodly smell you were letting out. I don't think I will be able to taste food for a week." Mr. Fields states because he can still taste the farts in his mouth. He walks off as Tonka yells behind him.

"I was challenged. Even the homeless want my crown, but I had to take her down." Tonka brags.

Dread woman is still on the train. She is climbing back up to a seat.

"He is wicket man. Me Say wicket man." Dread woman states.

CHAPTER SEVENTEEN:
FIRST BLOOD

Daren and Jennifer are entering a diner. The diner is not the kind you would dress up for, but they picked it because the food is good. Daren and Jennifer walk over to a table where three ladies are sitting. They are all teachers, but they don't look like teachers. They look young and out to have fun; however, when they talk, they sound just like school teachers. They are the gossip queens. Jennifer would not hang with these people under normal circumstances, but when she is at work, she loves to gossip. She does not gossip at church or with her neighbors, but at school it seem like she must be in the know.

"You see. I told you the men would not show." Daren states, as the ladies wave.

"They may be using the bathroom. Come on dear." Jennifer states as she urges him on.

"They don't all go to the bathroom at the same time. What do you think they are, women? I'm going home." Daren states as he stops walking.

"Don't be rude. At least say hello." Jennifer pleads as she grabs his arm to bring him over to the table.

"Hi everyone. This is my husband, Daren." Jennifer says as Daren waves.

The ladies all say hi and Daren and Jennifer sit down. As Daren got closer to them, he realized they were older then what they looked.

"I see you got your man to actually come." A brown skin skinny lady says. Her name is Sharon. She works in the office as a secretary.

"Yeah." Jennifer states.

"So did you all hear about what happened between the Principal and his personnel secretary?" A Caucasian lady states. She has a medium waist, but her cheeks look like she had smoked too many cigarettes. Her name is Dora.

"I heard, but from an unreliable source. Who did you hear it from?" A heavy set Jamaican teacher asks. Her accent is slight, but she still had enough of it where you can tell she is Jamaican. Her accent really came out when she got excited. Her name is Brenda.

"From the Janitor." Dora states.

"Well I heard it from the secretary herself. We are good friends." Sharon replies.

"You did, well spill it." Jennifer states. She joins in the conversation with excitement, forgetting all about Daren.

"I can't, she made me swear not to tell any body." Sharon states as if she is going to keep her mouth closed. "Oh hell yawl ant nobody."

They all start laughing, as they lean in close to gossip. Daren gives off a sigh. He whispers in Jennifer's ear. "Can I go now?"

"No, just a little longer." Jennifer states, and then hurries back to hear the gossip. She listens eagerly, only pausing to order her food.

Daren pouts a little. He sees the grapes on the table and puts on a sneaky smile. He starts eating it strangely. He takes one grape, and bites off the skin, by peeling it away with his teeth. When he finishes, he takes tiny bites out of the grape, as Jennifer's co-workers are looking at him strangely.

Jennifer hits him, but he keeps doing it. He sees some cheese doodles in a bowl, and starts eating them with small bites. It takes him about seven bites to finish one doodle. He also takes a long time chewing. The food comes, and Daren starts eating his food with his hand. He also chews with his mouth open, and even burps. Jennifer looks at him angrily. The ladies are looking at him and whispering to each other.

"Excuse me." Daren states.

"Why are you saying excuse me, and you didn't burp that time?" Jennifer states.

Daren looks at her and smiles. "Yooooouuuuuu know whhhhhyyyy."

The ladies and Jennifer gasp for air, as they cover their noses.

"That is foul." Brenda states.

Dean looks at Jennifer. "Can I go now?"

"Please." Jennifer states with a look of disgust on her face.

Daren walks out happily. Jennifer is looking frustrated, as the ladies are looking at her and whispering.

The next morning, Dawn is letting herself into Dean's apartment with a key. She just got home from her date wit Barry, and wanted to check to see was Dean still up. She sees Dean and Cheryl on the couch cuddled up. She takes a long hard stare at them, and shakes her head in disbelief. They wake up when Dawn slams the door close. Dawn walks over to the TV, and turns it off.

"Well, well, well. It seem like you both had a cozy night." Dawn states.

"Not as cozy as you. You did it to us again." Dean answers.

" I'm sorry." Dawn states.

"That gets tired real fast. You could have at least told us." Dean replies.

"I wanted to, but I knew you would be mad, and I didn't want to disappoint you." Dawn tries to explain.

"Well look how happy I am, but I'm cool with it though. Cheryl and I had a good time." Dean states.

"I don't mind, we can hang tomorrow night, or Monday since it's a three day weekend." Cheryl states, trying to calm things between Dean and Dawn.

"I'm sorry, but I'm going out again with him tomorrow night."

"Ok then, whenever. I'm out of here. See you two." Cheryl leaves, not wanting to get mixed up in their tension.

"Bye girl. I'll call you later." Dawn yells to her.

"See you Cheryl. Call me, we'll hang out sometime." Dean yells to her.

Dawn looks at Dean, as Cheryl closes the door.

"You two exchanging numbers now?" Dawn states with an attitude on her face.

"It's just a friendship thing. We had fun last night."

"Fun huh?" Dawn states looking at him. "I don't know why I'm trippin over this."

"I don't know why you trippin either." Dean states.

Dawn walks over to kiss him, but then pauses. "Were you kissing her because I don't want to kiss Cheryl. She's my girl, and all, but I don't get down like that." Dawn states.

"No I didn't kiss her. If you wanted to know, then you should just ask."

Dawn goes to kiss him good morning, but Dean pulls away.

"What?" Dawn asks.

"I don't want to kiss Barry either." Dean replies.

"Fair enough. You up for breakfast?"

"No, I'm going to sleep."

"You sure, I'm treating." Dawn states.

"No thanks." Dean answers.

CHAPTER EIGHTEEN: THE ART OF WAR

It is morning at Daren and Jennifer's home. Jennifer is talking with Carmen, in the living room.

"I know he didn't. Your husband is crazy." Carmen states as she starts to laugh.

"Yeah, and he had the nerve to fart on top of that." Jennifer replies.

"And where is he now?"

"He went to get us breakfast, but he'll be back here soon."

"Well then let me tell you about his friend, Tonka. That man had me hollering." Carmen states with excitement.

"Get out of here. You got him?" Jennifer asks.

"That man had me hoarse. I had to have me some tea with lemon in it. I told you I'll figure him out.

"You don't have him totally." Jennifer states.

"Yeah that is true. I got to eat out of his plate." Carmen rubs the hand that was pierced with the fork. "But that won't be easy."

Carmen soon leaves and Daren comes home with breakfast. He hates getting breakfast, but figures he will make it up to Jennifer before she declares war. He noticed her hardly talking to him, but he hopes breakfast will be a peace offering.

After breakfast, Jennifer is talking a little more, so they decide to go to the mall. Daren gets a little worried because Jennifer is not saying much in the car. He figures he will buy her something special at the mall, and that will patch things up.

Daren and Jennifer are walking through the mall.

"You still are not speaking to me?" Daren asks.

"I'm talking to you, but what you did was wrong." Jennifer answers. "And breakfast is not enough to make up for it, but it's a good start."

"I told you not to bring me there."

"Now those hens will be talking about me for a long time. I'm going to get you back." She states simply.

"Let sleeping dogs lie honey. You don't want to mess with me. You know how good I am. Besides, those women are not your friends."

Daren is about to asks her what she wants so he can buy it for her as a gift. That would have patched things up, but two of Daren's co-workers call out to him, and come walking over to him.

"Hi. Imagine seeing you here." The first lady says.

"What you shopping for?" The second lady asks.

"What is up y'all? I'm just looking for some pants. You two hang together on your days off?" Daren asks them.

"Something wrong with that?" Lady two asks Daren, seeing he is joking with them.

"No, it's just that people will talk." Daren states jokingly.

"Shut up big head. Oh, I heard about that crazy case you got." Lady one says.

"It is terrible. The house has lice, and the children had it in their hair. It was popping off of them, so I had to take a few showers to stop scratching." Daren tells them.

Daren looks around like he forgot something. "Oh this is my wife, Jennifer." Daren looks around for her, and sees she is hiding her face. "Jennifer, these are my co-workers. Why are you hiding?" Daren asks.

Jennifer never looks them directly in the face. She has mascara around her eye, making it look like she has a black eye. She acts shy and reclusive. They shake her hand, but look at her face. They are social workers and know the sign of a person who has been abused.

"I can talk now master?" Jennifer asks Daren.

"Master what are you talking about?" Daren asks her. He is confused by her behavior.

"Hello ladies." Jennifer states as the ladies get a good look at her face.

The two co-workers look at Daren. They walk away shaking their heads.

"Oh I'm going to get you back for that." Daren states, but Jennifer just laughs.

"Just a sample of what you did to me last night. Let's call it even, and enjoy the rest of our day." Jennifer states.

"Yeah, well you keep this up, and you're going to get a real black eye." Daren responds.

"Yeah you try it." Jennifer states as they get up in each other faces.

Later, Jennifer is getting food at a concession stand. Daren is sitting down, with a half open a ketchup package in his hand. She comes back, but just before she sits down, Daren throws the half open ketchup

114

package on her seat. Jennifer sits down on the ketchup, and has on white pants.

"Look. This is a peace offering. We each got each other, so let's let it be." Jennifer states.

"I hear you." Daren answers.

"So you accept my peace offering."

"Food, when have you known me to turn down food?" Daren asks.

"That is good because you know I would have won. I'm too smart for you." Jennifer states with a smile.

Jennifer moves a little in the chair to get comfortable.

"That you are." Daren states as he smiles, but he is careful not to let Jennifer see him. He knows he should have made peace, but he can't let her get away with it. He did it mostly because it is too good an idea to let go. He knows how bad this could turn out, and that she will get him back, but he still had to do it. The idea just came to him one day as he was coming home from work. He was thinking about it for a while and this was just the occasion to try it out.

Daren and Jennifer throw their left over food in the trash. They start walking, and Jennifer takes Daren's arm.

"Now isn't peace much better than war?" Jennifer asks.

"Oh yeah."

A couple passes Jennifer from behind, and looks at her in disgust. Jennifer looks back at them like they're crazy.

"You see the look they gave me?" Jennifer states as she wipes her face. "Do I still have mascara on my face?"

Daren looks at her face. "No you don't have anything on your face." How does he keep such a straight face? No one knows.

Two young ladies pass her from behind, and look at her. They start laughing. Jennifer sees it.

"Now what's that about? Those heifers don't know me." Jennifer says.

"No, I think they are laughing at me." Daren states. "Or maybe because you have on white, after Labor Day."

They continue walking. An old lady gives Jennifer some tissue. Jennifer takes it.

"Thank you. You see I do have something on my face." Jennifer states as she wipes her face. She looks at the tissue, but sees nothing on it.

"Oh, you just have a little something under your lips." Daren lies, as Jennifer wipes her chin area. She can't see people behind her looking at her butt.

"Did I get it?" Jennifer asks.

Daren looks at her face. "No you still have a little more."

Jennifer wipes again. "What about now?"

"You got it." Daren stated.

Jennifer throws the tissue in the garbage. A young lady approaches her.

"I know how it is girl. I have an extra one in my purse. Here." The young lady says as she passes her a tampon.

"What's this for?" Jennifer asks her.

The young lady nods her head slowly. Jennifer looks at the back of her pants, and she sees a big red stain by her lower buttocks. She looks around for Daren, but he is gone.

"I'm going to kill him." Jennifer says angrily.

Jennifer makes her way to a pants store. She sees a sales lady.

"I need a pair of pants." Jennifer states to her.

The Sales Lady looks at the back of her pants. "I can't let you try on pants with your monthly leaking like that."

"It's a stain. Aaaaauuuuugggggghhh!" Jennifer yells.

As she changes, she thinks of the many ways she can get revenge. Exlax in his soda, but they just ate. Plus Daren would never take food from her, after what he just did. He wouldn't trust her.

"This is going to go too far." She thought. Then again, he made people think she had her monthly. That will have to be avenged. Besides, if she let that go, he will think he won.

A few minutes later, Jennifer is talking on her cell phone with a new pair of pants.

"I am not going to hit you. Just tell me where you are, pay for my new pair of pants, and we can go home like nothing never happened." Jennifer states in a low voice.

"No. I would feel more comfortable if we remained in public for a few hours." Daren states over the phone.

"Then meet me by the concession stand." Jennifer asks.

"By the security office." Daren says over the phone.

"OK, that is fine with me dear." Jennifer answers. She hangs up her phone, and walks through the mall. She picks up some lemonade on the way.

Daren is sitting down as Jennifer approaches him.

"I had to buy these pants." Jennifer stated.

"That is understandable." Daren answers, ready to make the peace. He knows how deep this can get, but wants to quit with him ahead.

Jennifer sits down next to him, and then spills her drink into his lap. Daren jumps up, as Jennifer starts yelling.

"Oh no, you wet yourself again. That is the third time this week. You need professional help. How could such a small penis produce so much water?" Jennifer screams so everyone can hear her.

Daren never saw that coming. He has to find a way to turn this around. Everyone is looking at him, but he looks around, and starts rocking. He looks at the ground, and speaks like he is mentally challenged.

"I'm----sorry--please---don't hit---me." Daren states loudly, as he cowards away in shyness. Everyone starts looking at Jennifer, as Daren runs to the bathroom.

"There is nothing wrong with him. He is faking it." Jennifer tells them, but the people are still looking at her. She gets so frustrated she yells, "Aaaarrrrrggggghhhhh!"

Daren comes out of the bathroom after drying off his pants.

"Now we are even. Can we stop now, and enjoy the rest of the day at the mall?" Jennifer asks him.

"That is what I've been trying to tell you all along, but you will not stop." Daren states.

Jennifer takes his arm, as they walk through the mall. She laughs to herself.

"You are crazy. You had me wondering why those people were staring at me." Jennifer says. She stops at the window of a store. "Oh I want to look in that store for some blouses."

They walk in the store. Jennifer looks at a blouse, and puts it up to her.

"How do you like this one dear?" Jennifer asks.

"I don't like the color dear."

"I'm going to try it on anyway dear." Jennifer states as she walks to the dressing room.

"Then why did you ask me, dear?"

Jennifer is heading for the dressing room. She stops and looks back at Daren.

"Watch my purse, it's by you." Jennifer tells him.

"I'm not watching a ladies purse." Daren replies.

Jennifer goes to the dressing room, and then a few minutes later, she comes out with the shirt in her hand.

"What happened?" Daren asks with his hands up in the air.

"I didn't like the way it looks." Jennifer replies.

"I told you." Daren brags.

"Oh come on. Let's look in another store." Jennifer takes her pocket book, and then she looks at Daren. "Now honey, you know I'm too smart for you. I thought you said you were going to stop." Jennifer states with a smile.

"What?" Daren plays innocent.

Jennifer looks in her pocket book, and pulls out a blouse, Daren stuffed in there. She puts it back on the rack.

"You want me to walk out the store, the alarm goes off, and then you accuse me of stealing. Be nice. You promised." Jennifer states calmly.

She is happy she had caught him before he had a chance to execute his plan.

"Yeah you got me this time." Daren answers. "I just could not resist."

They both walk out and the alarm goes off. Jennifer looks at Daren sharply. Daren starts yelling.

"Oh no. She's stealing again. I'm getting tired of this. Every time we come to the mall, she takes something different." Daren states loudly, and with a whine in his voice.

A crowd gathers, as Security stop both of them. Security asks them to go through again. Daren goes through and there is nothing. Jennifer looks at Daren before she goes through. Jennifer goes through nervously, and the alarm goes off. The security blocks her, and asks to look in her bag. They do, and find a substance in a plastic bag, which looks like weed. They look at Jennifer.

"That is not mine. I don't know how it got there." Jennifer tries to explain.

"Sure you don't. We will have to call the cops." Security one states. He is a large man well capable of holding her. Jennifer sees that it is useless to struggle.

"Did you see what she stole?" Security two asks.

"She did not steal anything. She had a security sticker on the bottom of her pocket book." Security one states because he had already checked.   "My husband is playing a trick on me. He is---." Jennifer tells them, and then looks around for Daren, but he is gone again. The police come and handcuff her. They take her away despite her protesting.

Daren is window shopping at a sporting goods store. He sees the merry-go-round, and walks over to watch the children. There are a lot of parents with their children. Suddenly, two children approach Daren, and start yelling. "That is the man. That is the man that was touching our private area. That is him."

Some people look at him, as parents start grabbing their children closely.

"These children are lying. I don't know them." Daren states, but to no avail. Some men walk over to Daren, and he walks away. They start to chase after him, and he runs off. The boys who accused Daren are seen with Jennifer, and she gives them five dollars a piece.

Minutes later, Jennifer is walking up to the car, and Daren is sitting in it. Daren's shirt is ripped. Jennifer gets in the car smiling.

"You almost got me beat up." Daren states. The men had chased Daren, but he was able to get away from them. One of them was fast enough to grab his shirt, and that is how it got ripped.

"Well I was handcuffed, and would have gone to jail if a cop had not recognized it was tea in the bag, and not weed." Jennifer states. "You go too far."

"You started it." Daren answers her as he drives off. He gives smart looks to those who are looking at his ripped up shirt.

"Just like a child." Jennifer states.

CHAPTER NINETEEN:
GHETTO MOM KNOWS BEST

Dawn is sitting on her couch, in her apartment. Barry, who is built like a football, has brown skin, with a bold hair cut. He is not usually Dawn's type, but he managed to charm her into dating him. Dawn really likes the attention she gets when she is with him. Dawn wanted to be an actor when she was younger, because she loved the attention the stars got. Once she flew to Hollywood, thinking she had talent. She would have gotten the part, but she had to part with her panties to get the role. Dawn was not about to spread her legs to get ahead. She went back home, went to college, and got into advertisement. She would never regret her trip to Hollywood, but she would always tell her friends that she learned to get by on her brains, and not her looks.

Barry makes her tingle inside is what she would repeat over and over to Dean. She is attracted to Barry, and has love for him.

Barry had worked hard all his life to be the best. Football never came easy to him. He had to start training earlier then the other children, and work out longer. He watched his hard work pay off in college, as he was picked to go pro. He figures his hard work has earned him the right to have a lady like Dawn at his side. He has a crew of ladies that is ready to replace her if she slips up. He receives big bucks for going pro, and is expected to be rookie of the year.

"So why do I have to meet your mother?" Barry asks.

"Cause I want you to meet her." Dawn replies.

"Is she coming out with us?" Barry asks.

"If she wants to, but sometimes my mother can act very funny. She may want to go, but then again, she may want to stay home and rest."

"Then why do I have to meet her. Mothers hate me." Barry tells her.

"She won't hate you, she just won't like you. I told her all about you, besides, I also want you to meet Dean."

"Oh yeah the guy you talk about all the time."

"I do not." Dawn states.

A knock is heard at the door. Dawn gets up to answer it. She opens the door, and an old lady, with a black wig over grey hair, is standing there with her legs crossed. She is wearing glasses. She looks nothing like Dawn. She has dark skin, and is a little tough old lady, who still lives in the Ghetto. Drug dealers and robbers do not bother her because she knew most of them when she was young.

Dawn goes to hug her, but sees her, and waves her back.

"Move away from me girl, let me concentrate." Mom firmly states. She has found herself in this position too many times. Too much soda and too long a ride to the apartment. Dawn is embarrassed, but what can she do. She knows it is best she stays out of the way. Barry starts to go to her to say hi, but Dawn waves him away. Mom inches her way to the bathroom, with her legs still crossed. She pauses for a few seconds to rock. Dawn starts to speak. "Mom you------."

Mom holds up her hands. "I said let me concentrate girl."

Mom takes a few deep breaths, and then she runs to the bathroom. Barry is looking at Dawn strangely.

"She'll be right out." Dawn states.

The toilet flushes, and the water is heard running. Mom comes out of the bathroom looking exhausted.

"Whew, those water pills will get you. I tell you that was a close one." Mom states.

"Water pills?" Barry whispers to Dawn.

"For her high blood pressure." Dawn answers.

"Hi mom." Dawn states as she hugs her mother.

"Hi baby. Oh look at you. Are you getting enough to eat? You're starving yourself." Mom tells her.

Barry gets up and comes over to her. "Hi." Barry holds out his hand. Mom looks at it.

"I don't like him." Mom states.

"Mom." Dawn says with a frustrated look on her face.

Barry puts down his hand, and Mom walks over and sits on the couch.

"Here we go again." Dawn says because she knows her mother does not like too many people; although, she loves to intimidate people, especially Dawn's boyfriends.

"What kind of fool puts out his hand to his girlfriend's mother? What are we making a business agreement?" Mom states. "Dang fool." She continues, as she looks at Barry. Hopping he would challenge her, so she can unleash her full wrath. Barry does not take the bait.

"Mom I got a feeling if he would have hugged you, you would have complained about that." Dawn states.

"Yeah I would have, but he didn't know that. He tried to shake my hand." Mom answers.

Barry comes over to her. "I apologize." He tries to hug her. Mom pushes him away.

"Too late now, fool." Mom barks at him.

Barry throws up his hands.

"Mama." Dawn says as if she was a child again.

"Don't Mama me. I want to eat, I'm hungry." Mom states.

"Let me call my friend. I want you to meet him." Dawn states as she goes to the phone.

"I don't feel like meeting a hundred different people. I want to meet some chicken or maybe a turkey or something. Can you introduce me to that?" Mom rudely asks.

Dawn gets on the phone anyway. "Dean, comes over. I want you to meet my mother, and my lover. Stop it. Come on over. OK, I'll see you soon."

Dawn walks over to the door, and Dean enters. She kisses him on the lips and Barry looks on in shock.

"This is my mother." Dawn says as she leads him over to Mom.

Dean walks over to her. "So that is where you get your beauty from. How are you?" Dean lies.

Dean gives her a big hug and a kiss, as she pushes him away. Dean does not mind, he continues to hug her.

Mom mumbles, as she pulls away, "Don't be up all on me like that. I'm too old for you young man."

"Oh cut it out. You remind me of my own mother, grumpy, but that is alright." Dean states.

"I noticed you didn't shake my hand. Why?" Mom asks.

"Why should I, did we make a business deal or something." Dean states.

Mom and Dean start laughing. Dawn looks down, and away. She then drags Dean over to meet Barry. Barry stands up.

"This is Barry." Dawn states with a smile on her face. They shake hands. "What's up fan?"

"I'm not a fan. I hate football." Dean answers.

"Why?" Barry asks.

"I don't watch football, but I hear you're good."

"I see you got a few moves of your own." Barry states as he looks at Dawn real quick. Dawn gives him a look telling him to stop it.

"Let's keep it cozy player." Dean states.

Barry laughs, and Dean smiles.

"Player, that is funny." Barry states as he looks like he wants to hit Dean.

"Mom, Dean and I were stuck in the elevator together." Dawn explains, trying to break the tension.

"So this is the nice gentleman that took care of you in the black out." Mom states.

"Yeah, my hero." Dawn answers, but looks over to see what Barry is doing. Barry is upset, and she goes over to him.

"Well what kinds of food do you like Dean?" Mom asks.

"I'm not coming out to eat with you." Dean answers.

"That is not what I asked you." Mom states sharply.

"Ok-Ok. Calm down. I like Soul food."

"Good. You are going with us then, and you will be my date. I will not accept no for an answer.

126

Mom, Dean, Dawn, and Barry are eating dinner in a nice soul food place.

"This food is good. I like these ribs." Mom says.

"These ribs are good, but they are not half as good as Dean's ribs." Dawn announces.

"He can cook. All I have to hear now is that you give a good bunion massage, and I'm taking you home with me."

They all start laughing except for Barry.

"Well time for me to give some back. I'm going to the bathroom." Mom states as she gets up and leaves.

"Yeah I have to go too." Barry says as he leans over to Dawn. "Ask him while I am away."

Dawn nods to him, and Barry leaves. Dawn leans on Dean's chest, closes her eyes, and talks with Dean.

"There is my pillow. I am tired." Dawn states.

"If your boyfriend could see you, you would be in trouble." Dean says, wanting to hear her response.

Dawn pops up for a second.

"Why? Cause I'm leaning on your chest. I do that all the time, and he is not going to mess with that." Dawn states, firmly. "Plus he wants me to ask you to take Mom off our hands."

"So you want me to take Mom home, while you two go somewhere romantic."

"Yeah. So you're going to do it or what?"

"I'll do it because I know I can't control what you do, but it hurts. It hurts me a lot to see you go somewhere with him." Dean states.

"It's not my intentions to hurt you. I'm just following my heart." Dawn tells him.

"I know you don't mean to hurt me, but I don't think you know what you want in life." Dean states.

"Why do you say that?" Dawn asks.

"Because there is no way in hell, you would be my girl, and kiss another man on the lips." Dean states.

"He knows we're just friends, and I used to do that with Blue all the time. You're a good friend Dean. You love me, yet here you are making a way for me to be romantic for another man. That is why I love you. Your sacrifice is not going unnoticed." Dawn says.

"It will always go unnoticed." Dean states with a sad look on his face. "I'm starting to loose hope."

Dawn looks at him, as Barry walks out and sees Dawn lying on Dean's chest. A few people stop him for autographs. Dawn sees him, but does not move. Mom also comes out. Barry comes over and sits down. He nudges Dawn a little and she moves over to him.

"Mom, Dean is going to take you home." Dawn states.

"Where are you going?" Mom asks.

"Mom, I'm grown." Dawn answers.

"And I will whip your grown ass. Where are you going?" Mom asks again.

Knowing she is crazy enough to do it, Dawn answers her. "I'm going to the beach for a walk."

"I want to go to the beach." Mom states.

"Why don't we do this? We all go to the beach, and you two let me have Mom to myself. We'll take a cab home." Dean states as he looks at Dawn.

"Why can't we all stay together?" Mom asks.

"I want to find out what a goofy child Dawn was. I can't do that with her around." Dean tells her.

"Well I have a lot to tell you son." Mom laughs.

"Please wait until I'm not around." Dawn pleads as she gives Dean a smile.

The song, "The beautiful one" comes on. The song by Prince that Mariah Carey and Dru-Hill re-made.

Dean hears the song, and starts singing. "This is the jam."

"I feel like a dance before we all leave." Dawn states.

Barry cuts in. "I'll dance with you dear."

"Come on." Dawn replies as she leads him to the dance floor. Dean is singing the words, while looking at Dawn and Barry dance. Dawn looks at Barry, and then lies on his shoulder. She then looks over at Dean, who is looking in her eyes. Dawn smiles at him. Dean does not realize Mom is looking at him the entire time. Mom gets up.

"You can't win it, if you're not in it. I'm getting in it. Bye Nigga." Mom states.

"What?" Dean asks a little confused. Mom walks on to the dance floor. Dean thinks for a second and follows her out on the floor. Dean dances with Mom, and they are right next to Dawn and Barry. Dawn and Dean again look at each other. Dawn's head is on Barry's shoulder, but she is looking deep into Dean's eyes. Dean is saying the words of the song to her. Mom lets go of Dean, and walks up to Dawn and Barry. "Barry, may I have this dance? After all, you may be my new son-in-law."

"Mom." Dawn says.

Barry looks at Dawn and starts smiling. "Sure. I didn't think you liked me."

"I don't. Now come on." Mom answers.

Mom turns Barry's back to Dawn, as Dean is already standing next to Dawn. Dean holds out his hands, and she comes to his arms. They dance close together. Mom keeps Barry's back to them. Dean looks into her eyes, and is saying the words to the song in her.

"I hear you singing." Dawn whispers to him.

"Yeah, but you don't feel me." Dean replies.

"I can hear you." Dawn states, but does not get it.

"But do you feel me?"

Dawn realizes what he is saying, and looks into his eyes. Dean puts his hand low on her waist.

"You feel me?" Dean asks again.

"I feel you." Dawn whispers.

They stay dancing and looking into each other's eyes.

"It's ironic." Dean states.

"What?"

"I can hold you so close, and yet your heart is so far from me. Your going to marry him one day?"

"Hopefully." Dawn states.

'I can see it in your eyes you really love him."

"I have been trying to tell you."

"I know. There comes a time where every ones faith is tested. I just can't believe any more." Dean looks her in the eyes, and gently kisses her upper lip. He pulls away slightly, and then kisses it again. He then looks at her and says, "Good-bye Dawn."

Dawn grabs his arm as he walks away. "What do you mean good-bye. You sound like your leaving me for good."

"No, I'm going to sit down."

130

"Something in your eyes scares me. It feels like your letting me go."

"I am in a since. I realize we can never be."

"We can still be close friends can't we?"

"Yeah, of course. It's just the lonely needs love as well."

"Then find you someone, but just leave time to spend with me."

"I will." Dean states as he is about to go sit down. Dawn grabs him again.

"And we can still finish this dance, can't we?"

"Yes we can."

Dawn looks into his eyes. "I don't like the look in your eyes. I can feel your hurt, but I can't do anything about it. I don't get to chose who I love." Dawn states.

"Neither do I." Dean replies.

An hour later, Mom and Dean are finished soaking their feet in the ocean. They are now sitting on a bench.

"That salt water probably did your bunions good." Dean tells her.

"My feet feel great." Mom answers.

"So what was she like as a child?" Dean asks.

Mom thinks for a few seconds. "Dawn? Well she had a sad life. She never trusted many people because people were always letting her down. It started with her father, that low life. He would make promises to her, but would never keep them. She would stand by the window all day waiting for him to take her to the park or the arcade or a movie, but he would never be there. He wouldn't even call. It didn't matter that I would take her to these places.

She was a beautiful child. Boy, the boys would give her all types of attention, but she would always have this sadness about her. When I would ask her about it, she would say she was lonely. I would ask her why because she has all these friends. I mean even the girls wanted to hang with her to be popular. I remember her saying the saddest thing I have ever heard a young girl say. She would say, 'Mama they like my looks, but no one can see my soul. I have so much more to offer.' Sad isn't it."

There is a quiet pause as Dean stares out into the ocean.

"Did you know Blue?" Dean asks. Mom smiles a little.

"Yeah, Dawn told you about him. She used to talk of marrying Blue when she got older."

"She said he saw her soul?" Dean says like a question.

"Yeah, he did. He loved her." Mom states sarcastically.

"He did for real or not?" Dean asks a little confused.

"You're serious?"

"Yeah, aren't you?"

"She didn't tell you?" Mom asks.

"Tell me what?"

Mom shakes her head in disbelief. "Blue was her imaginary friend. She would pretend he was there when her father would not show up." Mom states. Dean thinks for a while.

"What? She told me she used to kiss him on the lips every time she saw him."

"She did, but it was all pretend."

"But she told me he got shot."

"No. It was her who almost got shot. A boy who loved her tried to kill her when she wanted to end it. She found out he was selling drugs and wanted no part of him. He could not take the rejection, and shot at her. He was aiming for her head, but hit the tree next to her. Dawn ran and so did he. He was caught, and went to jail for attempted murder.

Dawn was a mess. The drug dealer paid for a good lawyer, so Dawn had to testify as the trial went on for months. He eventually went to jail, but was released a few years ago, and is far away from here. Dawn was deeply traumatized by the incident. She has been wary of men since then." Mom states.

"I wonder why she always wants to kiss me on the lips and lay on me." Dean asks.

"I don't know about the kissing part, but when she was younger, she used to lay on her father likes she lays on you. Yeah I know you like her." Mom states.

"Yeah, I'm doing real good too. The girl I love looks at me like a father. She once told me, being with me would be like sleeping with a brother."

"The way you two were tonight, you're not doing so badly. Oh an old timer like me knows these things. I see her all Goo-goo eyes over this Barry, but you hang in there. Keep doing what you're doing. You may win her yet. Love is different things to different people. To her it is dependability. She is not so much in love with Barry as she is testing you." Mom explains.

"Testing me for what?"

"To see if you will be there for her, no matter what. That is love to her." Mom answers.

"Mom, I love your daughter, with all my heart." Dean states with a serious look on his face.

Mom moves her hand as if she is getting ready to say something important. "First of all, I'm not your mother." Mom jokes.

"Mom! Stop playing." Dean states. "Man, you're like a ghetto Mammy homeboy."

"Just joking dear. Now where was I? Oh yeah. There is a saying I heard years back. It says, Cupid is Stupid." Mom states.

"Dawn said the same thing to me." Dean states.

"Cupid is Stupid. You hear what I'm telling you. For instance, you're in love with my daughter, and I also believe my daughter loves you. Falling in love is not a right, it's a privilege." Mom states.

"Shouldn't it be a right?" Dean asks.

"No. Sometimes it just happens, but most times you have to fight for it. And this isn't the movies boy, so you may not get the girl in the end. Most times it doesn't work out. That Cupid is Stupid. That is why you'll see a dumb guy with this sophisticated lady. You're wondering to yourself, how did that happen? Or you will see the tallest man you ever seen, with the shortest lady you ever seen, or a fat lady with a real skinny man. You know why that happens? Cupid is Stupid. Sometimes the right people fall in love, sometimes the wrong people fall in love. Sometimes the right people fall in love for the wrong reasons, and the wrong people fall in love for the right reasons. Sometimes it ends for the right reasons, and sometimes it lasts for the wrong reasons. You feel me." Mom states.

"I can't continue on like this because seeing her with him hurts." Dean tells her.

"You young people. Who told your generation love always feels good. You ever heard of no pain, no gain. It's supposed to hurt sometimes. It's always the people who are close to you, who hurt you the most. Now I'm not talking about a man or women physically abusing a person. My man tried that with me, and I kicked his ass out." Mom states.

"I don't know is it worth it all." Dean answers.

"Well that is for you to decide. You have to figure it out how much love is worth to you? If you could put a price on Dawn's love for you, how much would it cost? How much would you pay?" Mom asks him.

Dean is seen staring into the ocean pondering the thought of it. Mom is not expecting an answer.

CHAPTER TWENTY:
YOU CALL THAT MAKING UP?

Daren is in the showers singing a Paul Simon song, and the bathroom is steamed up.

"People think she's crazy she got diamonds on the soles of her shoes. Well that is one way to lose these walking blues, diamonds on the soles of your shoes." Daren sings.

Jennifer is getting a bowl of water from the freezer, which has ice cubes in it. Jennifer takes the bowl into the bathroom, and then over the shower. Daren is still singing.

"She says honey take me dancing, but they ended up by sleeping in a door way, by the lights and the bodegas on upper Broadway. Wearing diamonds on the soles of their shoes." Daren sings.

Jennifer pours the water out on him.

"Aaaaaaahhhhh. Girl, I'm going to get you." Daren screams, as he falls down in the shower. Jennifer runs off.

"That is it; I'm going to get you. You know I hate cold water." Daren states.

A few minutes later, Daren comes out the shower with some cut off sweats he uses as pajamas.

"I have had it. You and I are going to have it out." Dean tells her.

Daren sees Jennifer in some tight spandex shorts, and Jennifer is looking very sexy in them. Daren is looking at her.

"Like I said, you and I are going to have it out right now. Get in that bedroom." Dean states.

Jennifer walks over to him and they start kissing.

"Truce?" Jennifer asks.

"You play dirty girl, but truce." Daren agrees.

"I'm going to get out of these clothes, so meet me under the covers in five minute." Jennifer states as she runs to the bedroom.

"Five minutes? What's going to take you so long? Let me come and help you." Daren yells after her.

"Five minutes." Jennifer yells from out of the bedroom.

Daren sits a timer right in front of him. He does a few push ups, and stretches like he is getting ready to run. As soon as the bell sounds, he takes off for the bedroom. He opens the door and gets under the covers, where Jennifer is. Daren kisses her neck, but Jennifer stops him.

"Honey, you left the door open."

Daren continues to kiss her. "So?"

"Baby, you know I can't do it with the door open."

Jennifer always felt like someone is going to walk in on her, and catch her. Even though no one else is in the house.

"Why? We're alone here." Daren states.

"I just can't."

"Then close it."

"You close it, you left it open." Jennifer states.

"Yeah, but you want it close."

"I'm not going to close it."

"I'm not either." Daren states.

137

"Ok, we don't want to argue about it. Let me just give you a sample.

Jennifer reaches over and grabs his erect penis, and starts rubbing it. Daren jumps up so fast he trips, but gets back up quickly. He closes the door so hard it re-opens, and he has to go back and close it again. He jumps back into bed.

"Now where were we?" Daren asks.

Daren kisses her on the lips, and she stops.

"I smell garlic on your breath. Why didn't you brush your teeth?" Jennifer asks.

Daren puts his hand up to his mouth and smells his breath.

"First you threw the water on me, then I came out, you were like five minute to sex, and I couldn't think, so I forgot." Daren explains, as he looks at her for mercy. He sees none, and says, "I'll be right back."

As he leaves the room, the phone rings.

"Don't answer it, I'll be right back." Daren states.

Daren pours a lot of tooth paste on to his toothbrush, and brushes his teeth quickly. He then rinses. He searches for the mouthwash, and rinses his mouth. He then rushes back to the room, and sees Jennifer on the phone.

"So she did what when she caught them?" Jennifer asks the person on the phone.

Daren lets out a sigh. He then motions to her to hurry up. She sees him.

"Ok. Sharon, I got to go. No I got to go. I'll hear the rest tomorrow. What? I know he didn't." Jennifer got caught up in the gossip from her co-worker at work. Jennifer sits up in bed, as Daren lies down beside her. He starts rubbing on her vagina, and it starts to get wet. She moves his hand, because she doesn't want to get into it on the phone. Daren leaves the room frustrated. He starts playing his video games in the living room.

The clock on the cable reads 11.PM. The clock then shows 11:40 PM. Daren checks the phone, and he still hears talking. He sighs, and continues to play his game. The clock reads 12:10 AM. He checks the phone, and hears the dial tone. He jumps up, but checks his breath first. He then goes to brush his teeth again. He enters the room, and Jennifer is knocked out. Daren clenches his teeth in anger. He lies down, turns on the TV, and starts flicking through the channels. He stops on one channel, and sensual music and moaning is heard. He turns the channel quickly. He stops on another channel.

"See how the male mounts the female."

The TV. states, "As the male Lion is seen mounting the female lion."

Daren turns the TV. to another channel. He looks at Jennifer who is still sleeping. He turns the TV. up loud, but she is still sound asleep. He gets out of bed.

"Jennifer." Daren calls.

She remains sleeping. He calls a little louder. "Jennifer."

There is no response. Daren then jumps on the bed real hard, and Jennifer jumps up and looks at him. She wipes her eyes. "What's wrong with you?"

"What do you mean?" Daren asks innocently.

"You shook the bed." Jennifer states sleepily.

"No you were having a nightmare, but now that you're up." Daren states as he starts kissing her.

"Baby, I'm tired." Jennifer states as she lays her head down.

"Well let me get a quickie. You know I can be quick when I want to." Daren tells her.

"Yeah I know that, but I'm tired. I'll hit you off in the morning." Jennifer states.

"All you got to do is arch your butt up, and you don't even have to move much." Daren begs as he demonstrates it by arching his butt up.

"I am going to sleep, now leave me alone." Jennifer states.

"Ya tease." Daren states. Jennifer looks at him, and then lies down to sleep. Daren watches her, and then turns on the light. Jennifer jumps up.

"What now?" Jennifer asks.

"If I can't sleep, you can't sleep." Daren states.

"You're sick, you know."

Jennifer storms over to his side of the room, mumbling angrily. She turns off the light. Jennifer goes back to her side, gets in bed, and settles down. Daren turns the light back on. Jennifer covers her face with her covers. Daren sees her, and pulls the cover off of her. She sits up and screams.

"Uuuuggggghg." Jennifer screams with frustration.

Daren and Jennifer both start watching TV. Daren looks at Jennifer, and is about to say something. Jennifer never turns her head. She just speaks. "No." Daren stops what ever he was going to say, and turns back to the TV.

"And now for the sexual habits of the king cobra." The TV stated. They are both seen turning their heads to the side to look at the screen. Daren points to the screen and looks at Jennifer.

"I said no." She says firmly.

Daren turns around and angrily kicks out his covers. They go back to watching TV.

"The cobra got no arms or legs and he's getting some." Dean states.

"The cobra is one big dick like you." Jennifer answers.

"Yeah I got your big dick."

"What---ever." Jennifer states.

CHAPTER TWENTY ONE: THE STAND OFF

Daren and Jennifer are lying in bed. Daren turns to her.

"It's morning." Daren states.

"I know. You kept me up all night." Jennifer replies.

"But you said you would hook me up in the morning."

"You have got to be crazy."

"So when?" Daren asks.

"NEVER!" Jennifer screams.

Daren jumps up. "If there is one thing I can't stand. It's a liar. I'm going to rake the yard." Daren states.

"Good, maybe I can get some sleep before Church." Jennifer says, as she closes her eyes.

Daren is raking the yard violently. Gary sees him from the gate.

"That is truly a sexually frustrated man." Gary states to himself. He calls out to Daren.

"Hey, boo-boo. What's the matter Boo-boo?"

Daren looks even more frustrated. "My name is not Boo-boo. It's Daren. I told you to stop calling me that."

"Ok. Boo-boo. Sit down and talk with me." Gary states.

Gary puts his hands around him and sits him on the stairs. He sits close to Daren.

"Gary." Daren states looking straight ahead.

"Yeeesssss." Gary answers.

"I'm not homophobic, but--Get your arm off of me, and move the hell over." Daren orders him.

Gary jumps to the other side of the steps.

"Maaaaaannnn, we are testy this morning. First raking the hair out of that poor grass, and then attacking me. Now I know the signs." Gary states.

"What signs?" Daren asks.

"You know what I'm talking about. I've been going through the same thing since Thane left me. It's been four weeks." Gary says.

"Is there a reason you're here?" Daren asks.

"You mean why I'm alive? Oh yeah. You have built up tension. The wife is holding out on you, right." Gary asks.

"What's it to you?" Daren asked.

"I can help you."

"Oh hell no. You done lost your mind." Daren stated.

"Not that, ya silly."

"What then?" Daren asks, confused.

"You can get her the same way she got you. Music." Gary states.

"You're nuts."

"I should be if you are what you eat. I done ate enough of them, to be one." Gary jokes. "No seriously. One day she played anthem music, and had you and a few people cleaning the yard. It hyped you up to do it. You can get her to make up with you by using music too." Gary states.

"What music?" Daren asks.

143

Gary pulls out a tape. "Play this and you got her. We women fall for this every time." Gary answers as he looks down the block. "I can't believe this. Here comes Thane riding down the block on a bike." Gary states. He looks at Daren. "Do me a favor, and wave to him."

"I'm not waving to him." Daren states.

"Just wave to him. Come on I helped you." Gary begs, and puts his hand on his arm. "Pllleeeeaassse?"

"Ok. Just keep your hands off of my arms." Daren states.

As Thane bikes by, Daren waves to him. At the same time, Gary yells hi to him, and puts his arm around Daren.

"Thane. Yoo hoo- Thane. This is my new man." Gary states.

Daren puts his hand down and starts chasing Gary, who runs to the edge of the gate. Daren punches at him, but Gary catches his arm and twists it. This bends Daren over in pain.

"Ooowwwww. Ok. You got it." Daren states.

"You damn right I got it, and I'm going to take it."

"Let me up." Daren tells him.

"No. Not until you say, 'I love you Gary."

"Hell no. You just have to break my arm." Daren answers.

"Ok. Ok. Say Aunty."

"No."

Gary twists his arm harder.

"Ok. Aunty." Daren states.

Gary lets him up and then runs up the block.

"You better run." Daren states as he looks around to see if anyone saw it.

Later that morning, Daren and Jennifer are arguing in the car, as they are going to church.

"You got me going to church all tired. " Jennifer complains.

"If you would have done what you promised, you would be going to Church happy, instead of grumpy." Daren states.

"Well you better romance the hand, because that will be all you're getting for a while." Jennifer states.

"Please, I'll break you easily. You will be begging for it by the middle of the week." Daren replies.

"I will last a lot longer than you will. You! Ha! You will be bothering me after Sunday school." Jennifer replies.

Daren parks the car and gets out, as they start yelling a little louder.

"Bother me tonight, and see won't I get you. I'll leave if I have to." Jennifer threatens.

"So leave. You're not doing me any good any way. Just dead weight." Daren states.

"You are so stubborn. A stubborn fool." Jennifer tells him.

"That is it. It's official. I can't stand you." Daren answers.

"I can't stand you. I should have never planned to give you none." Jennifer replies.

"Well I should have never married you." Daren shouts angrily.

Jennifer stops and takes a long look at him. "I hate you." Jennifer states.

"I hate you too." Daren replies.

"Don't you speak to me ever again." Jennifer says, as they open the door to the church. They see the people, and they both say hi to them all friendly, like nothing is wrong.

"How are you two today?" The Pastor asks.

"Fine." Daren and Jennifer both answer, with a fake smile. When the Pastor walks away. "I can't believe you said that." Jennifer states. She is obviously hurt.

"I though you said don't talk to you."

CHAPTER TWENTY TWO:
FROM RUMBLE TO HUMBLE

Tonka is seen dropping Dean off at Dean's apartment. Tonka is eating an ice cream cone, and Dean is getting out.

"Thanks for the lift Tonka." Dean states.

"No problem. The movie was cool. We all need to hang like this." Tonka says. Dean leans on the car's passenger door, from the outside.

"Yeah, that would be cool, but the trouble is getting us all together. I haven't spoken to Daren or Jason since we all ate out. I would not have met you had we not bumped into each other." Daren says.

"Yeah. I heard from Daren, but no one has heard from Jason. That is unusual." Tonka replies.

"Yeah, he is always looking to hang out or something."

From behind, Barry taps Dean, and Dean turns around. He sees Barry with two of his football friends. Barry and his friends are much larger than Dean, but Tonka gets out of the car and walks over to Dean. Barry looks at Tonka, but focuses on Dean.

"I see what you're doing. Yeah I see you getting in good with the mother, and making goo-goo eyes at my girl." Barry states.

"What the hell is goo-goo eyes?" Dean asks sarcastically.

"She loves me, and you have better stay out of my way. You have nothing to offer her. I have fame and fortune to place in her lap." Barry states.

"Funny." Dean answers.

"There is nothing funny here." Barry states.

"You didn't say love. You don't even love her." Dean states.

Barry grabs Dean. Dean tries to struggle, but Barry's friends hold Dean.

Tonka is seen thinking, as two clouds appear over his head. One cloud shows him helping Dean by stopping them from hitting him. The other cloud shows him eating his ice cream cone. He shrugs his shoulder and the clouds disappear. He then goes back to licking his ice cream cone.

"Let's take him to the alley, and work him over." Barry states.

"You had to bring friends, huh?" Dean states as he is struggling.

They drag Dean behind the building, and Tonka walks with them. Barry looks at Tonka.

"Hey, this ant no peep show punk, beat it."

Dean looks on, hoping for something to happen.

"Come on." Dean whispers to himself.

Tonka looks at him, and Barry pushes him. Tonka falls back a little. The clouds appear again. On the one side Tonka is beating up the three men. On the other side there is Tonka eating an ice cream. Tonka shrugs his shoulders, and the cloud disappears. Tonka goes back to licking his ice cream cone. Barry and his friends are about to beat up Dean. Barry sees Tonka is still there, and he walks up to him again.

"I told you to beat it." Barry states, as he knocks the ice cream cone out of Tonka's hand.

"Yes" Dean states to himself, as the ice cream cone falls to the ground like it was falling in slow motion.

Tonka looks at the ground, and then at them. He charges Barry first. Barry braces himself, but hits the wall hard, and has the wind knocked out of him. One of his football friends charges at Tonka by getting in a football stance. Tonka gets in a football stance as well. They charge each other and the friend flies up in the air, and lands on his back. He is out. The other friend charges, but Tonka flips him over his back. He hits the ground hard.

Tonka walks up to Barry. Tonka points at Barry, and Barry points to himself, (as to say, who me.) Tonka points towards Dean. Barry points at Dean. Tonka shakes his finger no. Tonka points to the ice cream on the ground, and Barry points to the ice cream on the ground. Tonka shakes his finger no, as to say don't mess with. He then makes a fist with both hands, and tries to crack his knuckles. Nothing happens. He tries it again, strains, and then farts. He then has a surprise look on his face.

"Dean, can I use your bathroom, it's an emergency?" Tonka runs to the front of the building, as Barry jumps out of his way. Dean goes to open the door to his apartment.

"Thanks Tonka." Dean states, as Tonka runs by him to his bathroom.

A few hours later, Dawn is in Dean's apartment talking.

"He really tried to jump me with his friends." Dean tells her.

"I knew he was jealous, but I had no idea he would try something like this. I'm going to talk to him about this. We have a date tonight." Dawn states.

"Do what you want." Dean replies, a little frustrated that she is still going to see someone who tried to jump him.

"My mother left this morning. She said she had a good time with you." Dawn states, and then continues. "You know you caused an argument."

"I did, how?" Dean asks.

"Barry was upset because I was laying on you." Dawn states.

"That is your fault, not mine."

"You know I felt what you were saying in that song." Dawn tells him.

"No you didn't. If you did, you would be mine." Dean says.

"I feel you, but Barry makes things go off in me when I kiss him."

"Then why do you like lying in my arms?" Dean asks.

"All I can say is your arms feel right, and comfortable. I look into your eyes and understand that you will be there for me." Dawn states.

"I desire you. You don't feel that for me?" Dean asks.

"I don't understand it." Dawn replies.

"I don't understand it either."

"Look, boyfriends come and go, but friendships can last forever. You think I'm going to throw away what we have just to have sex with you. You add sex and tongue kisses, and everything gets messed up." Dawn states.

"So if I was to have a friend I would spend time with, how would you feel about that?" Dean asks.

"That is fine, as long as she doesn't interfere with my time with you. Cause just like I told Barry. No one is going to come between Dean and I." Dawn states.

"Then you do not love Barry?" Dean asks, surprise she told Barry that.

150

"Who knows what love is. I get goose bumps when I am with him. Does that mean I love him? No. What about when I don't get goose bumps with him? Does that mean I stopped loving him? Dean you have to know. There will never be intimacy between us, but there will always be love and friendship." Dawn states as she leans over to him, and pecks him on the lips. "That is unique to me." She tells him.

"What about your father? Your mother told me a little about him." Dean changes the subject.

"I don't ever talk about my father to anyone. OK. baby." Dawn states softly

"My bad. I didn't mean anything by it." Dean states.

"I know you didn't." Dawn says, as she hugs him.

"Now this feels right to me." Dean stated.

"It feels right to me too."

"Yeah, but your rightness is not the same as my rightness. Your mother is right." Dean states.

"About what?"

"Cupid is stupid." Dean replies.

"She has been saying that for as long as I remember." Dawn states.

Dean stops hugging her.

"I'm going to start my dinner." Dean states.

Dawn pulls him back to her. "Wait, just hold me a little longer." Dawn asks.

Dean holds her, but looks in her face, and can tell she is tearing. "What's the matter?" He asks.

"My father was ---He was a terrible man." Dawn states.

"Baby he can't pay for his mistakes forever. Let it go." Dean states.

"Then how long will I have to pay?" Dawn asks.

"Until you let it go." Dean states.

"I know you think I am crying over my father, but It's not just that. I feel strange, like these times will not last long. Just promise me that who ever you may meet, date or even fall in love with, won't take away time from me. I just need your friendship." Dawn pleads.

"I promise." Dean states.

CHAPTER TWENTY THREE: BRAIN VS. PENIS, AND THE WINNER IS--

Dawn is sitting on her couch dressed. She is waiting for Barry, who is running late. While she is waiting, she falls asleep. She wakes up, and realizes that Barry is not going to show. She then wants to be near the one who will make her feel better. She gets up, and tries to enter Dean's apartment, but the door is locked. She opens the door with her key, and enters just past the door way.

"Dean? Dean, you home?" Dawn yells into the apartment, but she can tell no one is home. She leaves. She enters her apartment and picks up the phone. She calls Cheryl, but she is not home. She sits back on her couch, and ends up falling back to sleep.

Dean and Cheryl walk into Dean's apartment. Cheryl goes to the bathroom. Dean called her earlier and asked her out dancing. He figured Dawn was out with Barry, so he did not even try her. The thought of her screwing Barry was too much for him. He had to get out, and so he called Cheryl, who agreed. They went out to eat, and then decided to go dancing. Cheryl is a good person to hang with. She is funny, cool, and knows how to dance. He did not think about Dawn all night.

Cheryl has other plans. She put on her best dress, and did her make-up flawlessly. Dean could not take his eyes off of her butt all night. She kept looking back to make sure he was looking. She didn't ask him to dance during the reggae songs for nothing. That lump in his pants told her she was doing her job. Now she had made an excuse of having to use the bathroom to get into his apartment.

Cheryl comes out of the bathroom.

"Wow that was fun. Who knew you could dance." Cheryl states.

"Yeah that was fun. You want something to drink?" Dean asks.

"No, I'm good. Hey. How come you don't have a girl? I mean you're a nice guy, a good date, and should have a girl." Cheryl states.

"For the same reason you don't have a man. People don't recognize a good thing."

"Sometimes a good thing is right under your nose, and you don't even know it."

Cheryl comes by him, and start dancing reggae in front of him, even though there is no music on. She turns around and places her butt right against him. Dean puts his arms around her, and she moves back even more.

"What am I doing?" Dean states. "I love Dawn.

"I know, but she loves Barry, and I'm feeling you."

Cheryl turns around, and rubs her hand against his penis.

"I think you like me as well."

"Baby that is lust, and it is not the same." Dean states, but does not move her hand.

"Well can I try to change your mind." Cheryl states, as she kisses his lips.

"Damn, they are soft. She may not get tingles, but I sure do."

Cheryl pushes him down on the couch. She goes to kiss him again. She then sits on top of him, and start kissing him. Dean stops.

"You know I love her. My body is with you, but my heart is with her. Maybe we shouldn't do this." Dean states.

"I know, but she has her man, so give me a chance. You're not attracted to me?" Cheryl asks knowing the answer. She reaches down and feels his penis. "This guy is saying yes. All we need now is a yes from you."

"I don't know." Dean states.

"I know you get lonely, because I can feel your loneliness now." Cheryl whispers in his ear.

"Yeah, but what is this we're doing?" Dean states.

"I have feelings for you. I see how good you treat her, even if she doesn't. If she wants you, I will step out of the way, but she is into Barry, so let me have this night. Just give me one night to change your mind." Cheryl states.

"I don't know." Dean answers.

"Let me play something for you." Cheryl states as she gets up. Cheryl goes to his CD. player, and plays "Give me tonight" by Will Smith-

Cheryl starts dancing in front of Dean and looking at him. She pulls him up. They both start dancing close.

"So can I have tonight, just one night out of the rest of your life?" Cheryl asks.

Dean starts kissing her, and in his defense, he never had a chance. Her dress, her personality, and it have been a while; He is caught, and doesn't mind being caught.

Cheryl pushes him on the couch again, and sits beside him. She is kissing him, as he starts rubbing her breasts. He starts over her clothing, and then pulls out her breasts. He breaks between kissing her to suck on her breasts. He can hear her heavy breathing, and it turns him on. She reaches down to his pants quickly, and unbuttons them. She zips down his zipper, and pulls out his penis. She usually starts rubbing it through the pants first, but she had felt its form on the dance floor, and wants to feel it in its purist form. Dean ran his hands up her stocking to her vagina. He starts rubbing the area where her vagina is and can hear her breath change. She starts to moan, and kisses him harder. He rubs her harder. He starts to feel her wetness through the stockings and her panties. She stands up, and takes off her stocking and underwear.

"Leave the dress on, that shit turns me on." Dean states as he takes this time to slip on a condom.

She sits back down, and he reaches for her vagina again. Her vagina is so wet it is wetting the sides of her legs. It feels so soft, as he felt from the bottom first, and then worked his way to the click. Cheryl is going crazy rubbing his penis. She is too excited. Her rubbing is actually starting to hurt. Dean brings his hand, which he was using to rub Cheryl's vagina with, to his nose. Once he sees that she has no bad odor, he wants to eat that wet pussy out. Cheryl is way ahead of him, as she already started sucking his erect dick. Dean lies down opposite her, and she gets on top of him, putting her pussy right in his face. She is tearing his dick up. She sounds like a wild animal the way she is moaning. Dean starts eating her wet pussy. He starts with the sides, and sticks his tongue deep into the pussy, but he knows what he has to do. He goes straight for the click. Cheryl is going crazy. He could not see her face, but he believes she is crying because it feels so good. Her moans excite him so much, as he circles over her click. Occasionally he would dip into the pussy. He takes a finger and starts pushing it slowly into her butt hole. Cheryl goes crazy, and stops sucking his dick. She is moaning so loud, Dean is sure he is going to hear it from the neighbors. She then goes back to sucking his dick. She is sucking so hard it felt like a vacuum cleaner. Dean heard these loud screams, and sees her body slow up a little. He takes note that her pussy starts tasting salty, and knows she has cum. She keeps sucking him, and he grabs her to let her know he is cumming. She is still breathing hard, when she looks at him like wow. He is trying to be cool about it, but he knows that was incredible. Cheryl sits on the couch, and Dean goes to his knees and starts to eat her out again. She opens her legs in welcome, and soon the moans start again. She gently grabs Dean's head, and starts moving her hips. She closes her eyes, and turns her head from side to side, getting into it.

Dawn is sleeping on her couch. She wakes up suddenly. She looks at the time, and goes over to Dean's apartment. She figures he has to be home by now. She opens the door, and sees Dean and Cheryl on the couch having sex. She is on top of Dean riding him.

They stop when they see her. She looks at them with such intense hatred, that her lips quiver. Dawn runs up to them, instead of out of the apartment. Dean is putting on clothing, as Cheryl has on her dress, but no underwear.

"You two are fucking each other." Dawn states angrily.

"I though you were hanging out with Barry?" Dean states.

"He didn't show. You are supposed to be there for me, not fucking my friend. Whatever happened to I will always love you?" Dawn asks.

"I have nothing to explain to you or be sorry for. Do you ever think about me when Barry is fucking you? You're just mad because you got a taste of your own medicine. How does it feel? My world can no longer revolve around you. I can't follow you around while you date who you will. You think I'm going to wait for you forever, but I have my needs." Dean states.

"I'm the stupid one because I believed all of your lies. I'll be there for you, but that was bunch of crop." Dawn states as she is pacing the room. Cheryl is standing there watching them.

"I am there for you, but you are never there for me." Dawn states.

"It's Barry who is not there for you, but you still worship him. You know what? I see the real you. The inside you and you know what? I don't like it. You are selfish, self centered, and care nothing about anyone else's feelings, but your own." Dean states.

Dawn starts crying. "How dare you say that about me. Our friendship ends now."

"Give me back my house key." Dean states. Dawn takes the key of off her ring. She throws it at him.

"You broke my heart tonight." Dawn states. "You really broke my heart . Worse than Barry ever could have."

"Now you know how it feels. Just think of how many times you have done it to me." Dean answers.

"I'm out of here." Dawn states. She looks at Cheryl. "Can we talk?"

Cheryl gets up to go with her. Dean takes Cheryl's hand. "She will be over later. We have something to finish."

Dawn storms out.

A half an hour later, Dawn is sitting on her couch crying. Cheryl enters and sits on the couch. Dawn holds her head up without looking at her.

"You finished what you started?" Dawn asks with anger.

"You damn right I did." Cheryl answers. "And you need to know that it was me who pushed up on him. He kept saying he loved you, but I know he was in need.

"How can you betray me like that?" Dawn asks.

"You betrayed yourself." Cheryl answers.

"What are you talking about?"

"You told me that you two are just friends. I did not know, before tonight, that you are in love with him. On the phone you would talk about Barry, and state that you and Dean will only be friends." Cheryl states. "We did nothing wrong because he is not your man."

"I know that, but—" Dawn tries to say.

"But what? He did nothing wrong. We did nothing wrong." Cheryl states.

"You don't understand. He betrayed me." Dawn answers.

"You can't betray what's not yours. Why didn't you tell us how you felt?" Cheryl asks.

"It's not that, it's-----It's just that—" Dawn tries to say.

"What? You can't think of anything can you?" Cheryl asks.

"No I can't." Dawn states.

"Then why are you so mad?" Cheryl asks.

"I don't know. Seeing you two together like that flipped something in me. It caught me off guard."

"He has no right to tell you don't have sex with Barry, right?" Cheryl states.

"No." Dawn answers.

"Then you can't tell him who he can or can't have sex with. Look you need to love him or let him go. You can't hold up a perfectly good Black man, and not use him." Cheryl states.

"I don't feel with him what I feel with Barry."

"I don't care what you say. You love him. Now that I am sure of that, I won't touch him ever again. Dean and I also agreed that would be best." Cheryl states.

"I am in love with Barry. He just could not be here for me tonight." Dawn states. "But you two are free to do what you want"

"Did Barry even call you to say why he didn't show?" Cheryl asks

"No." Dawn answers.

"Open your eyes and see that Barry is not the one for you."

"He is the right one for me."

"What are you going to do with Dean, leave him alone?" Cheryl asks.

"Dean is all yours. I won't go back over there." Dawn states.

"Good, then I 'm going back over there to get me some more of that good stuff. I'm going to win his heart, and show him all the love I can." Cheryl states as she walks out of the apartment, and closes the door.

Dawn waits for a while like she is going to bust. She starts for the door, and then stops. She then opens the door, and finds Cheryl is waiting there for her.

"You don't want me to see him again, do you?" Cheryl asks. Dawn looks at her, and shakes her head no. Cheryl hugs her, and then goes to leave. Dawn calls out to her, and Cheryl comes back.

"If he loves me so, then why did he sleep with you?" Dawn asks.

"Your answer is in another question. Why do you sleep with Barry? I gotta go, but please, don't play with his heart. Love him, or set him free." Cheryl states.

"Cheryl?" Dawn calls after her again.

"Yeah." Cheryl replies.

"Was it good?" Dawn asks in a whisper.

"He laid me down nicely." Cheryl states as she walks out of the main door.

"My mother's right." Dawn thinks to herself. "Cupid is a stupid, motherfucker."

CHAPTER TWENTY FOUR:
HE LOVES ME; HE LOVES ME NOT

Tonka and Carmen are eating at a restaurant. Tonka is eating his food fast. He finishes his food, and he looks around and sees Carmen still has half a plate of food. Carmen drops a napkin on the floor, so she bends down to pick it up. She comes up with it, but it falls from her hand again. She reaches and grabs it again. When she sits back up, her plate is empty, and Tonka has a mouth full of food. He is pretending he does not know what happened to her food. Carmen looks around, looks at Tonka, and even peeks on the ground to see if some of the food fell. She then looks back at Tonka.

Tonka and Carmen are walking down the board walk, eating ice cream cones.

"Want to taste mine?" Carmen asks.

Tonka shakes his head yes. He bites off most of her ice cream cone, leaving just a little of the edge of the cone. Carmen looks in amazement and smiles at him for a second. She looks at the tiny piece of ice-cream cone left, and throws it in a garbage can, as they are passing by. She looks at him eating his ice-cream cone.

"Can I have a taste?" Carmen asks in a sweet voice.

Tonka looks at her and shakes his head no. He protects his ice-cream.

"You shouldn't have eaten yours so fast." Tonka states, as he keeps walking. Carmen stands there with a blank look on her face.

CHAPTER TWENTY FIVE: JASON BUTTERFLY?

Dean is knocking on Jason's door. "Yo Jason, open up. It's Dean. Your boys have been worried about you."

A voice comes from the door. "Go away."

"Man, open this door before I knock it down." Dean States.

The locks are heard coming off the door. Dean opens the door, and sees the apartment in a mess. There are chips on the floor, and old Chinese food on the table.

"What's going on with you player? This ant your style." Dean asks, as he is looking around.

"Some serious mo-jo man and I don't know what's going on." Jason whines.

"Have you been out with girls?" Dean asks, but by the look of the apartment, he knew the answer.

"I was, but I don't want them no more." Jason states.

"I have never known you to turn down a pretty brown round. You sick or something?" Dean asks.

"I know man. Girls are calling, but I don't answer the phone no more. I even had a girl here naked, but I just didn't want it." Jason states.

"Who the hell is this before me?" Dean wonders to himself. He knows it looks like his friend, but he is behaving like someone else.

"You got it bad." Dean states.

"It's Tammy. I can't stop wondering who she is with now, but it should be me. I drive by her place, but it's dark, and I want to call her, but I'm scared." Jason states.

"Of what?"

"I'm scared of who might pick up the phone. I can't go back to her because I can't get that image of her, and that other man, out of my head." Jason states.

"She was good to you. Why don't we go over to see her?" Dean suggests.

"I can't because if she is with someone, then I will go crazy. Is this love? Is it supposed to feel this way?" Jason asks.

"I'm telling you, like this lady told me. Cupid is stupid my friend, but we don't have to be. Go see her." Dean suggests again.

Thinking about it, but missing the point, Jason states, "Yeah, it's true. Cupid is stupid. When I don't care about her, she is with me. When I start caring, then she is not with me. I have cheated on her many times, but she cheats on me once, and I can't forgive her. This love thing is crazy. I need to move to the mountains, and become a monk."

"Naw, you need a night out. Come on, it will be like old times. We just have to cleanup before we leave, so we can bring ladies back here." Dean states.

"You're hanging out now? What happened with the girl you were stuck in the elevator with? You moved into her building right?" Jason asks.

"We're just friends. She's dating Barry from the Giants." Dean states sadly.

"Get out of here, Barry. He is expected to be the best player in the game. Did you get his autograph?" Jason asks, excited.

"Picture me asking for an autograph. What do I look like, a fan."

"That is Barry the bear." Jason states.

"I don't even watch football. Come on man. Let's meet some girls at the club, and do our thing." Dean says.

"OK. I'll go get ready." Jason states. Dean starts cleaning, while Jason takes a shower and gets dressed.

Jason and Dean take a cab to a nearby club. As they enter, "It's getting hot in here" by Nelly, is playing. They immediately go to the dance flour.

Dean and Jason are seen dancing with different ladies on the dance floor.

"OK. You take this side, and I'll take the other side." Dean yells over the music to Jason.

"Remember get one for me, and I'll get one for you." Jason states, getting into the party mood.

"I'm not a rookie. I know how it goes. Hell I taught you." Daren answers.

A few minutes later, and Dean is talking to three ladies, at the bar.

"I'm a pharmacist by trade. I dropped a pill in each of your drinks. It won't make you pass out or go numb. Hell we got liquor for that, but this will make you horny as hell.

"How horny?" One of the ladies asks with a smile.

"Well put it like this. Here is my number. You call me if you need me." Dean states.

Jason is watching the dance floor. Dean comes over to him with Twins. They are light-skin, have a long weaves that looks nice, cherry lipstick, well proportioned bodies, and they wrapped all that up in tight blue dresses. They are one of the hottest items in the club, and Dean has pulled them. He doesn't know what it is, but when he is in the club, he is in his element. He could almost get a lady to do anything, but even he is surprised he has pulled these Twins. Dean saw his chance, threw out a crazy line, which showed he did not give a fuck, and it worked.

"This is Manash, and this is Jaytwa, but I'll share. Their idea of fun is switching up on their boyfriends." Dean states.

Jason takes one of their arms, and they both lead the ladies to the dance floor.

About a half an hour later, Jason brings two ladies over to Dean.

"Dean tell these girls who is over at our apartment right now." Jason states, as the two ladies listen with interest.

"You are not supposed to tell anyone." Dean states trying to look a little upset.

"They don't know where we live, so it does not matter." Jason explains.

"Good, because he said he did not want to be disturbed." Dean states.

"Who?" one of the ladies asks.

"Jay-Z-Jigga man himself." Dean states.

"Take us to see him, pleeeeaaaase. We won't tell anyone." The other lady begs.

"He may have stepped out. We never know when he is going out, but he always returns in the morning." Jason states.

"Take us there. We'll do anything for an autograph." Lady one begs. She walks close to Dean, and whispers in his ear. "Anything."

Jason and Dean look at each other smiling. Dean is happy to see his friend is back to his normal self.

Later, Dean and Jason are drinking and talking.

"So who you want to take home tonight?" Dean asks.

"Well I got a ton of numbers. The honeys are out tonight, but I think I feel like a double pleasure." Jason states. He looks at Dean and holds out his fist. "Double up?"

"Double up." Dean answers back as he gives Jason's fist a pound. "Let's tell the ladies they are the lucky winners, and blow this joint."

"Cool, let's do it. Let's go to your place. It's neater." Jason states.

"No yours, is closer. Besides, we cleaned up enough." Dean answers.

Forty minutes later, Dean and Jason are in the apartment with the Twins. They are both kissing the ladies. One on the couch, the other against a wall.

"I don't know what was in that horny juice, but it is working. Where is your bedroom?" One of the Twins asks Jason.

Jason points to a door on the other side of the room, and then says, "I'll be with you in a minute."

Jason comes over to the corner, and Dean goes over to him.

"What was in that drink you gave them?" Jason asks.

"It was just lemonade. Their own desires are doing the rest. The drinks just give them a reason." Dean states.

"I'm drunk as hell. You good on the couch?" Jason asks.

"Yeah you are drunk, because when have I not been good on the couch?" Dean asks.

"True. I'm going to do my thing." Jason states.

Dean follows Jason to his bedroom door, where one of the Twins is. He yells inside as well as looking at the Twin on the couch.

"You ladies better not switch up on us in the middle of the night. We can't tell you apart." Dean states.

One of the Twins comes out of the bedroom, and talks privately with the other one. They then start smiling as they part.

Dean and Jason look at each other, and both say, "Tichal-tichal."

Jason is about to go into his bedroom.

"Jason. Remember, represent."

Jason holds up two fingers. He goes from his private area, to his heart, to his lips, and then to the air. He goes into his room, and Dean sits down next to his Twin.

"Now why should I give you some on the first night?" She states with a smile on her face.

"Well, Why not?" Dean asks.

They both laugh, but she only laughs for a second. This means that she is half serious, and requires a good reason to give him some. Dean knows this, and knows better than to answer that question. A wrong answer might have her storming out of here, and leaving him with his dick hard. This would also mean her sister is leaving with her. Jason would tease him for years on how he ruins what was supposed to be their legendary night.

"Look. I'm going to turn down the lights a little, and what ever happens, happens. No pressure." Dean states.

"Good answer." He thinks to himself. If she does not object to him turning down the lights, and as long as he gives her the right compliments, he is in there. He has already kissed her, and that is all he needs to get her excited enough to touch her pussy. He knows that if the hand touches the pussy, then the dick is going to touch the pussy. It's just a given. This is one of the few times the dick and mind are working together. The dick for obvious reasons, and the mind is doing it just for the ego.

Dean turns down the lights, and returns to the couch. Dean starts gently rubbing her breasts and she moves his hand away.

The dick asks, "What is the problem?" The mind answers, "She wants to appear to be noble, so don't panic. She would not have come here if she did not want to do it. She just does not want to appear like a whore. Just keep at kissing, and try it again later."

Dean starts kissing her harder, and leaning his body against her. She starts moaning slightly. He waits about three minutes, and then starts rubbing her chest again. This time she pulls a breast out. They continue to kiss, and then Dean reaches for her vagina, but on the outside of her dress. He touches it, and she starts moaning louder. Thoughts of Dawn come into his head, but he puts it out. There is a prize under that dress, and he wants to reach it.

Dean thinks he hears something coming from the bedroom, but he thinks it is just Jason doing his thing. The moans get louder, and his worst fears are confirmed. Suddenly loud crying is heard from the bedroom, as Jason's voice is heard.

"Tammy. Where are you Tammy? I love you. I'm sorry, I can't do this any more."

Dean and the other Twin look at each other.

"I have to call for back up. This is serious."

About an hour later, Dean and Jason are on the couch alone. Jason is drinking right from the bottle, and is still crying.

"Maybe you should give me the bottle." Dean states as he watches his friend get drunker and drunker.

"No, this is all I have left. Tammy is with another man. I'm sorry the ladies left, but I couldn't sleep with her. I'm sorry to ruin your night." Jason apologizes.

Dean knows this is serious. He had heard Jason say he was passing on pussy, but he did not believe it. When he saw it with his own eyes, he still couldn't believe it. This night was supposed to be legendary. They were supposed to be eighty years old telling these other old guys how they mack these hot twins from the club. Dean is not mad at him because he knows they almost pulled it off. Hell they did pull it off, but just didn't follow through with the sex part.

Dean sits there listening to Jason saying how he couldn't do it, and Dean started to feel guilty about Dawn. Sure he is mad at Dawn, but how is he so willing to do something with other people. He justifies it by saying she is screwing Barry, and he still has his needs. That's how he justified Cheryl, but he was in great need then. He reasons that if he was with her, he would never cheat on her, but this is not the case. His thoughts are interrupted when Jason throws a statement at him that requires an answer from him. He does this in between his crying for Tammy.

"I didn't mean to spoil our big night." Jason states again.

"Don't worry about me. I didn't really want to do it anyway. I was also thinking about my own beauty Queen." Dean half lies.

There is a knock on the door. Dean opens it, and Daren and Tonka come in.

"I have never seen him like this." Dean explains to them.

Jason looks over and sees Tonka and Daren. "My dogs are all here. My dogs are all here."

"I got work today, so what are you doing Jason?" Daren states.

"I miss the only girl I have ever truly loved, and I was too stupid to see it." Jason states, as Daren and Tonka's face dropped. They have never heard Jason talk like this. Dean had told them how Jason was behaving, but they just had to see it for themselves.

"Why don't you give me the bottle" Daren states.

"No. I just need some air. Let's get out of here." Jason says.

"That is not a bad idea. We need to get out of this apartment." Daren agrees, as he looks at the others and they all agree.

CHAPTER TWENTY SIX:
CUPID IS STUPID

The men are sitting on benches, at the beach, talking.

"What's the matter with you Jason? You never pass on a girl." Tonka states.

Jason answers in a sluggish, drunken, pathetic voice.

"It's not me. It's Cupid, and he is stupid. He is sitting up in the clouds smoking La all day. He is laughing, and messing with our hearts and heads. When she loves me, I didn't care for her. I loose her, and she doesn't care for me, and now I love her. CUPID IS STUPID, and I hate him." Jason explains.

"I have never seen him like this." Tonka states as he turns to Daren.

"I have never been this way before, and I have never wanted anyone like this. I want my baby back." Jason states. He looks to Daren. "Daren, you're married. You have been all of our mentors. What do I do?" Jason asks.

"I know Tammy really loves you. She put up with your stuff for a while. She's a good woman, so you need to try to win her back." Daren states.

"I've cheated on her too many times, so she will never forgive me." Jason says.

"You will either win her back, or lose her for ever and move on, but you will not be this way for another second." Daren states as he looks at him sternly.

Jason takes a few deep breaths, and stops crying.

"Just go see her in the morning." Dean adds to try to encourage Jason

"What if there's a guy there?" Jason asks.

"Then you will still be respectful." Daren states.

"Daren is right. She loved you, and may love you still." Tonka states.

"What if she doesn't want me back?" Jason asks.

"Like I said, you move on. Use it as a lesson for learning when you enter the next relationship. The lesson is no cheating." Daren states.

"If you get her back will you cheat on her again?" Tonka asks.

"No way, I'm done with that. I couldn't even mess with these fly twins Dean and I brought from the club." Jason states.

"I believe you." Tonka says to him, and put his arm around him for a second.

"That is the truth." Dean states. "I witnessed it myself."

"What about that girl you like Dean?" Tonka asks.

"We're arguing now." Dean answers.

"She's dating Barry from the Giants." Jason tells them.

"The Bear? She's dating the Bear?" Daren asks Dean in disbelief. "Yo get me a football or an autograph." Daren asks.

"You have got to be crazy, if you want me to get an autograph from him. He has my lady. You should get Tonka's autograph, because he beat him up a couple of weeks ago." Dean states.

"Hey, he knocked over my ice cream cone." Tonka explains, justifying himself. "And you know how I like the cream."

"So what's up with you and this girl?" Daren asks.

"We had an argument because I can't take her stuff. She wants to mess with who ever she wants, but I can't touch another woman without her screaming on me." Dean states.

"What happened? Let's hear the entire story." Tonka says.

"She saw me having sex with her friend, and flipped, but she says she does not love me." Dean states.

"What are you doing having sex with her friend, if you love her?" Tonka asks.

"Come on Tonka. You think with your stomach sometimes, and I think with my other head sometimes. I was in deep need." Dean explains.

"Sounds like she loves you, but do you miss her?" Daren asks.

"I can't front. I do, but I'm mad at her now. She needs to stop using me as a doormat. If we are going to be friends, then we should act like friends." Dean states, knowing deep down inside he doesn't want to act like friends.

"I hear you." Daren states as he then looks at Tonka. "We have not heard from Tonka. What's up Tonka?"

"Man I have been chilling. This lady can cook, and she's cool." Tonka states.

Daren is thinking. "Here I am trying to give you all advice, and I am at odds with my own women. Look at us. All of us except Tonka are having love problems. Jason is right, Cupid is Stupid. Cupid is nothing but a damn crack head, selling love cheap, so he can hit the pipe." Daren states.

"Love and problems go hand and hand. At least you're married. This girl doesn't even love me. When we were in the elevator---" Dean begins to explain. About an hour later it is day break, and Dean is still talking.

"And so she storms out of my apartment." Dean finishes.

"I still say it seem like she likes you if she gets that jealous. She kisses you on the lips, but never gives you the tongue. Hum? I don't know because that is strange. I think she has some psychological issues." Daren states.

"Well, I'm going to stay away from her. She really got me mad this time." Dean tells them.

"Come on, you can't stay away from someone you love." Tonka says.

"I have to. She thinks she can do what ever she wants to me, but she has to learn to respect me."

"You hear Tonka. Hey Tonka when have you been in love? "Jason states.

"Love? Man you can't tell me nothing about love. You haven't been in love until you have had a sundae at Joe's." Tonka answers, as he licks his lips.

"Awww man." Everyone states at Tonka's comment.

"Tonka, what is up with you and Carmen?" Dean asks.

"What?" Tonka says back.

"You fallen for her?" Daren asks.

"I don't know. She has not said anything to me about love." Tonka states.

"Do you love her?" Daren asks.

"Who knows what love is. What is it a feeling, an emotion, or a notion?" Tonka states, throwing them the questions.

"It's different things to different people." Dean says.

"What is it then?" Tonka questions them.

"It's that feeling like you always want to be with that person, forever." Dean states with a distant look in his eyes.

"Like you feel now about Dawn? You don't want to be around her now. Cupid is Stupid like Jason said." Tonka states, as Dean is left without anything to answer back.

"I got this. It's like loving that person with all you got." Daren says.

"You can't describe Love the noun, with Love the verb." Tonka states.

"I mean love is like you want to sacrifice yourself, for that person." Daren continues.

"Oh like you want to sacrifice for your wife now. I don't see any compromises there." Tonka tells him.

"Ok you got me, Cupid is stupid." Daren agrees.

"Love is just a glorified form of like. It's our way of saying I like this person more than the others." Jason says.

"I think it's just a word, and not a feeling. I may love this person one minute, and be arguing with them the next. Where is that feeling then?" Tonka asks.

"It's still there, just deep inside, until it's time to make up." Daren states.

"Then it's all hopeless?" Jason asks.

Daren, seeing that it will soon be time for him to go to work, takes charge. "No it's not hopeless. Just because Cupid is stupid, that does not mean we have to be. I know we all have jobs to go to, so here is what we are going to do. Jason, you will go see Tammy this morning, before she goes to work, and will work it out. Dean, you go talk to Dawn, and make your peace with her. If she loves you, it will come out, so work it out. I'm going home to my wife. She may not be there when I get home, but this evening, I will work it out. Tonka work what ever is going wrong with you and Carmen, and you're not telling us. She's a good woman. Everyone in the car, I got to get to work." Daren states. "I can't take off after a three day weekend."

Everyone turns and head to the car.

"But everything is fine with me and Carmen." Tonka says.

Everyone gets in the car, and Daren takes off. He turns on the radio, and hears the song, "Loneliness won't leave me alone," by Sanchez.

Daren is thinking. He starts nodding his head to the song. He imagines Jennifer and him are in the car at the beach. He sees them walking along side the water, and dancing as if they can hear the music. The scene switches to their home, and Jennifer sticks her hand out of the bedroom asking him to come in.

Jason is bobbing his head to the music. He then starts to imagine. He sees himself knocking on Tammy's door, and she invites him in. She starts dancing with him, and they start kissing.

Dean is bobbing his head to the music. Dean imagines that he comes into his apartment, and Dawn is there waiting on him. She grabs his arm and motions like she is sorry. Her lips are seen saying I love you. She hugs him, and they start kissing. There is a ring at the door, as Dawn answers it. She sees it is Barry, and then shuts the door on him. She then runs back to Dean. They sit on the couch and stare at each other's eyes.

Tonka is bouncing his head to the music, and licking his lips. He imagines he is eating a hamburger with French fries at his favorite restaurant. Then he imagines the fries and hamburger become life size, and are dancing with him. They are rubbing up against his body.

CHAPTER TWENTY SEVEN: OUT THE POT; INTO THE FIRE

Carmen is seen waiting outside of Jennifer's front door. Jennifer opens the door.

"Everything is not fine between Tonka and me." Carmen just blurts out.

Jennifer looks at her and then rushes back into the house. She is running late. Carmen comes in, as Jennifer continues getting ready for work.

"What?" Jennifer asks.

"He won't share his food with me." Carmen states as she follows Jennifer into the bathroom.

"So buy your own food." Jennifer states sarcastically.

"It's not a matter of buying food. Food with him is intimacy. If he doesn't share his food with me, then he could never really love me." Carmen states.

Jennifer starts doing her hair in the bathroom mirror.

"Look he hits you off lovely, and spends time with you. What more do you want?"

"I want his love, and his hand in marriage. I want it all." Carmen answers.

"Well you can't have everything you want." Jennifer states. She is upset because she can't get her hair correct.

"I will get his love, and excuse you. You need to go in that room, wake up Dean, pull up that tired dress, and released yourself because you are way too backed up." Carmen states.

"He ant here. He left late last night after he got a phone call." Jennifer replies.

"Wait. My problem first, then yours. He doesn't love me like I love him."

Carmen sees Jennifer is having trouble with her hair, and takes the comb out of her hand, and start doing Jennifer's hair.

"Have you told him?" Jennifer asks.

"I cooked for him. You know I don't cook for no man, except my father."

"Have you told him you love him?" Jennifer asks again.

Carmen thinks, then states, "No, not in words."

"Then tell him." Jennifer states.

"Ok. I will, but I'm scared." Carmen says.

"Of what?" Jennifer asks.

"I swear to you. I am ready to marry this man today, but I am scared he will not love me back. This is it because my future is on the line." Carmen states.

"People don't always fall in love at the same time. His time will come." Jennifer tells her.

"I don't doubt that. I just hope he falls in love with me." Carmen states, as she finishes Jennifer's hair.

Jennifer turns to her and says, "You have never been rejected in your life, so you will be fine."

"Thanks, I'll walk with you, and then take the bus from the school." Carmen states. I didn't see your car out front, so I assumed Daren has it still.

They exit the home, and are walking down the street.

"So Daren did not come home, and you think he's cheating?" Carmen asks.

'No. Daren knows if he cheats on me, I will kill him. One of his friends probably had a problem." Jennifer states.

"Then what's wrong?" Carmen asks.

"We were arguing and he said he should never have married me." Jennifer states. She seems very hurt about Daren's statement.

"You know he doesn't mean it." Carmen reassures her.

"There is always a little truth in what Daren says. I think he is mad because I can't give him a child." Jennifer states.

"Stop it now." Carmen says, giving her a stern look.

"I'm serious. He is always trying to have sex with me. I like it, but it's almost every night. I think he is trying to have a baby, and I'm afraid he will get disappointed if we can't have one. I think he regrets marrying me." Jennifer states as she fights back the tears.

"You're wrong about Daren. He's a good man, and you know that. He loves you. Besides, it's when they stop having sex with you that you have to worry." Carmen states, trying to lighten up the conversation. It works because Jennifer laughs, but she starts right up again.

"Nothing means more to a man than his seed. I can't even do the basics of womanhood." Jennifer says.

"Girl, a baby does not complete you. Children are a part of a family; they don't make or break the family." Carmen states." I learned that in a tape called, 'Growing Children God's way.' By the Izzu family.

"When he said he wished we never got married, he meant that, and it hurts me. This love thing is hard as hell."

Carmen starts thinking about Tonka, "But its rewards are not measurable."

Carmen knows what she wants, but for the first time in her life, she does not know how to get it. Her clever tricks only get her so far, and she can't buy his love with money. She will have to earn this, and that scares her. It will be hard, but if she gets it, she will never let it go.

"What tricks have you for making your husband love you for who you are?" Jennifer asks.

"Now you know I don't get involved with marriages." Carmen states. "All I can say is that you are wrong about Daren, and you know this."

Carmen made it a rule not to mess with married men or to get involved in destroying a marriage. Her mother always taught her that marriage is secret to God, and is nothing to take lightly. She has always believed that. She saw her mother refer a woman to the Bible, when the woman was complaining about her husband. Carmen respected her mother for that.

Mean while, Dean gets out of Daren's car, and walks to his building. He is still in his party clothes. Daren's car pulls off, and he sees Dawn is standing in front of the building, looking very tired. She looks at him. He is about to say something to her, but continues to walk to his apartment. He knows Daren said to talk it out, but when he sees her, his anger is re-kindled.

"We don't have to be friends to at least say hi to each other." Dawn states to him.

Dean continues to his apartment. Dawn turns to him, and yells, "You have your wish. Barry and I broke up."

Dean does not look back, but pauses for a second to say, "That is only half of my wish." Dean continues to walk into his apartment.

"I can't give you the other half." Dawn yells back to him.

CHAPTER TWENTY EIGHT: KNOCK, KNOCK, GUESS WHO

Jason is knocking on Tammy's door.

"Who is it?" a voice states from behind the door.

"It's me." Jason states.

The door opens; and a beautiful lady is standing by the door. She is half Black and half Asian Her breasts are OK, but her butt is banging. She has on sweat pants, which she sleeps in. Her hair is in a scarf, but she still looks sexy.

"Can I come in?" Jason asks. Tammy walks in the apartment, and leaves the door open.

"I know you're wondering why I'm here" Jason states.

"It has crossed my mind. Especially since the last time you were here, I had to spend the night in the hospital, having tacks pulled out of my feet.

"And we can't forget about the guy you were with." Jason states.

"What do you want?" Tammy asks, getting frustrated with the conversation.

"I want----I want." Jason tried to say, but is looking around.

"I want to go to the bathroom." Jason says as Tammy looks even more frustrated.

"There is no one here Jason." Tammy states.

"Did you sleep with him again?" Jason asks.

"Why don't you tell me how many people you slept with?" Tammy asks with an attitude.

Jason starts yelling, "Yeah but you----." Jason pauses, as Tammy looks at him to finish.

"But you cheated----." Jason starts to say, but stops. Tammy looks at him again.

"Yeah?" Tammy states.

Jason looks at her, "You--You--You slept with him."

Tammy walks off and enters the bathroom. Jason goes and knocks on the door.

"Go away." Tammy states as she sounds like she is crying.

"I didn't mean to—I did not come here to---." Jason gives up, and walks out.

CHAPTER TWENTY NINE: I GOT A BIG MOUTH!

It is evening, as Daren enters the room, and Jennifer is already lying on the bed. Daren lies on top of her, and she tries to get up.

"Wait one second. I just want to say sorry for being a jerk these last few days. I don't want to argue no more. I want to make peace." Daren states to her.

Daren tries to kiss her lips. She gets up.

"Judging by the lump in your pants, you just want to make love. You're not sorry for anything." Jennifer states

"You're not supposed to withhold sex because you're mad at me." Daren states.

"I'm not. I have had sex with you before when I was mad at you. It's just you really hurt me this time." Jennifer says.

"Baby I love you, and you know that. You know I say things that I don't mean." Daren explains, but he sees that she is not listening.

"Come with me." He states, as he goes to the living room. Jennifer follows him reluctantly. Daren presses play on the tape player.

"It is not going to happen because this is not going away so quickly." Jennifer protests. The music plays, and it is Celine Dion's song from the Titanic movie.

Jennifer hears the music, and her lips start to quiver, as she looks at Daren. She listens to the words of the song as Daren holds her in his arms. They are by an open window as the music plays. Gary is seen by the window getting into the song. Gary sees Daren's hand, and reaches in to touches it. Daren pushes his hand away, without letting Jennifer see it. Gary looks at Daren, and says the words, "I forgive you," without making a sound. Daren closes the blinds. Gary listens by the window, and is getting into the song again. Inside, Jennifer starts kissing Daren.

"I love you baby. You know that." Daren states.

Jennifer shakes her head yes. She has tears in her eyes. The scene shows Gary listen to them from the outside. Jennifer's voice is heard outside.

"Let's go to the bedroom." Jennifer states.

Gary is making the ooooohhh sound, with his mouth. He gives the thumbs up sign.

"I'm ready my dear." Daren states tenderly.

"I know what you have been waiting for. I've been waiting for it too." Jennifer says with a sensual smile.

Jennifer starts walking, and Daren follows happily.

"Yes --yes. Man I got to thank Gary." Daren states.

Gary is outside waving his hands like "back away." He is moving his hand across his throat as to say, "Cut it," but he knows Daren can't see him.

"What do you mean thank Gary? For what?" Jennifer asks.

"I said that out loud?" Daren states, surprised at himself. He explains to Jennifer, "He gave me the song, and said it will help calm you down."

Gary throws up his hands and shakes his head in disbelief.

"You think you're slick. You're not getting anything, so you use a songs just to get what you want. You're not sorry, you just horny." Jennifer yells at Daren.

"But I love you." Daren states.

"Yeah from the waist down." Jennifer states.

"You're so stubborn, so forget you then."

"I know you hate me because I can't give you a child, but I can't change that." Jennifer says.

"What are you talking about? I don't care about that." Daren states, wondering why she brought that up.

"Yes you do, you liar. Get away from me, and go out and get it elsewhere, but you're not getting it here." Jennifer states, as she storms off. Gary shakes his head and leaves the yard.

The Song---"All women," by Linda Ronstadt, is playing from Dawn's apartment. Dawn peaks out the window and sees Dean entering the building. She then goes to her peak hole in her door, and sees him entering his apartment. She sighs by the door. She then goes to her CD. player and turns up the song. She sits on her couch and starts crying. A knock is heard at the door. She runs to it smiling. She wipes her face, and opens the door. She sees it is Barry with flowers, and she looks disappointed. Barry looks at her shocked, as she closes the door, in his face.

Dean is seen in his apartment, listening to the song. He peaks through the peep hole and sees Barry leaving Dawn's apartment door. He sits down on his couch and looks sad.

Dean gets on the elevator at his job. On another floor, Dawn races on to the elevator, but does not know Dean is on it, until she gets in.

She looks at him, but he keeps looking straight. She gets off before him, and lets out a sigh of relief when the elevator doors close.

Jason is seen lying in his bed looking at a picture of Tammy. He looks up again and wipes his eyes. He gets up, and he starts out the door.

Tammy is seen eating dinner alone, in her apartment. She picks up the phone and then hangs it up. She has a picture of Jason sitting across from her, and is looking at it.

Jennifer is on her bed crying. Daren hears her, and leaves the house.

Hours later, Tammy hears a knock on her door. She opens it to see Dean. It is not their thing to speak to each other's girl, but he felt he had to help his friend, even if his love life seemed to be lost.

"Hi Dean" Tammy states, but her face told another story. Her face has a puzzled look on it. She is wondering why Jason's best friend is visiting her. Her first thought is he wants to flirt with her. She rules out that thought as she lets him in the apartment. She knows Dean would not do that to his close friends; but all the same, she will sit as far away from him as she can.

"Hi Tammy. You know why I'm here." Dean asks.

Tammy, after hearing that statement, figures he is there to talk to her about Jason.

"Take a seat. Are you thirsty?" Tammy asks.

"No I'm good, thanks." Dean states, as he takes a seat.

"So why are you here?" Tammy asks pretending not to know.

"It's about Jason. He has it bad for you, and it is real. I know he has messed up in the past, but he seems serious this time." Dean states, hoping she would be happy to hear that, but she has a sad look on her face. Then her sad look turns to anger.

"He's changed huh?" Tammy asks.

"Yeah he has. I am hoping you will take him back." Dean answers.

"You can come by here to tell me that your friend has changed, but where were you when he was cheating. Did you tell him not to cheat?" Tammy asks.

"Sometimes." Dean states.

"Other times, you doubled dated with him and the girl he was cheating on me with." Tammy says. She is not yelling, but is speaking sternly.

"Jason is a grown man, and I can't tell him what to do." Dean answers.

"And I am a grown woman also, and you need to let me make this decision on my own." Tammy states.

"Look he is my friend. We were playing together on the streets long before you stepped on the scene. I'm not going to rat him out for no one, and to no one." Dean states getting a little upset.

"Then you should return to your friend." Tammy says as she gets up.

Dean gets up to leave. He is a little sad he did not achieve his goal. He walks to the door, and can see Tammy is hurt. He never thought about looking at this from her point of view. He understands that Jason was doing her wrong, and he told Jason; however, Jason will do what he wants, so he partied with him. No he did not consider that he was contributing to destroying a good woman. He knows Tammy will never trust another man for a long time to come, especially another Black man. He never thought about how many Black men will have to pay for Jason's promiscuity. On the other hand, he can not be responsible for grown people. Jason did what he wanted, and Tammy allowed him to. Something in him knew that he would never tell on Jason, but something in him also knew that somehow, this grown woman deserved an apology.

"I never saw it from your point of view." Dean states without turning around. "For what it's worth, I'm sorry." He says as he walks out. Tammy closes the door behind him.

Dean gets to the elevator, as he hears Tammy's door open.

"Dean." Tammy calls after him. He stops and turns, just as the elevator comes up.

"Thank you." Tammy states. Dean nods to her, and gets in the elevator.

CHAPTER THIRTY:
THE RE-EDUCATION OF TONKA

Tonka and Carmen are sitting on the couch, at Carmen's home.

"Tonka, I have something to tell you." Carmen states.

"Can we eat first? I am hungry." Tonka says, holding his stomach.

"Your steak is in the oven warming up." Carmen replies. She looks at him. "Tonka I want to tell you something."

"I'm listening." Tonka states.

Carmen looks him deep in the eyes. "I just want to say that I love you. With all my heart, I love you. I have never felt like this about any man, and it's sort of hard to say, but it is real. I love you, and want to spend the rest of my life with you. I know that is a bit strong, but that is how I feel."

Tonka looks at her, and kisses her on the cheek. "That is nice, dear."

Carmen looks at him, and waits for him to say something, but he doesn't.

"I'll go get your food, and bring it to the table." Carmen states.

Tonka sits there thinking for a while. Carmen's face is very sad as she reaches into the oven, which has a plate with food on it. She uses a pot holder to bring the plate to the table. She sits in a chair by his, and waits for him to come.

"Be careful it's hot." She states to Tonka as he comes to the table.

"You're not eating." Tonka asks.

"No. I lost my appetite." Carmen replies.

Inside she felt like she had lost much more. The first time she spills her soul to a man, and he ignores her. She figures she will fake a headache after he eat, and then be alone to cry. She did not know that Tonka did not believe in love

"Well I found my appetite and yours, and I'm going to use both of them." Tonka states as he laughs a little, but does not notice Carmen is not laughing. Tonka goes to sit down, and accidentally bumps the table. The plate falls off the table, but Carmen catches it. Carmen screams because it is hot, and puts the plate back on the table. Tonka is looking at her like he is so amazed. Carmen holds her hand, which is slightly burnt. She goes to run cold water over it, and Tonka goes with her.

"Are you ok?" Tonka asks.

"I think the tips of my fingers are turning red." Carmen states looking at her finger tips. She start waving her hand because of the pain.

"You saved my plate. No one has ever sacrificed themselves for my food like that." Tonka states, while looking at her in amazement. He takes her hand and kisses the burn area.

"Is that better?" Tonka asks as he looks into her eyes.

"No, it still hurts, but I'll be ok." Carmen states. She looks at Tonka and realizes he is not eating. She looks at him strangely.

"You're not eating?" Carmen asks.

"Forget the food, let me put some butter on your fingers. It will stop the stinging." Tonka states as he gets up and goes to the refrigerator.

Carmen looks in shock. "Forget the food? You feel ok."

"I'm fine, but you look different." Tonka states.

"How?" Carmen asks, not knowing if it is an insult or a compliment.

"I don't know. You're glowing more." Tonka states while he is looking at her smiling. He gets the butter and brings it to her.

Carmen blushes. "You're glowing. Now eat your food." Carmen jokes with him.

Tonka reaches over and kisses her on the lips. She is taken by surprise, but enjoys the kiss.

"Uuummm. What was that for?" Carmen asks smiling.

"That was a just because kiss." Tonka states.

"Can I get another one?" Carmen asks.

Tonka leans over and kisses her again.

"That was great, now eat your food. I want to talk to you in the bedroom later." Carmen states with a sexual look on her face. She forgets about using her headache excuse.

"We can do that now." Tonka states.

"Stop playing, you have to eat your food first." Carmen says. She is smiling so hard it feels like her face will crack.

Tonka takes a bite, and Carmen looks at her fingers. When she lifts her head up, Tonka has a piece of meat on his fork offering it to her. She looks at him, and eats off of his fork. Her lips are trembling, and she starts tearing. She reaches for a fork on the table, and is going for his plate. She hesitates, and rubs her hand that got stuck with the fork. She then goes for it, and takes some potatoes out of his plate. She starts laughing for joy. Tonka moves his plate over to share the food with her, and she starts eating. Tonka looks at her.

"I'm hungry, but not for food no more." Tonka states. Tonka starts kissing her. She starts crying.

"What's the matter?" Tonka asks.

"I have waited so long to eat from your plate." Carmen replies.

"You can have my plate. I want you." Tonka states as he takes her by the hand to the bedroom. She breaks free, and grabs the whip cream.

"You won't need that anymore." Tonka states.

This time is even better then the last time. Carmen is in bliss because she ate off of Tonka's plate.

Tonka loses so much weight in the years to come. He hardly wants food anymore, but he bothers Carmen almost every night. She does not mind, because his attention and love is on her.

CHAPTER THIRTY ONE:
PAPA WAS A ROLLING STONE

It is evening, and Dean is walking into his building with an elderly man. The man has on a suit, and flowers in his hand. The man has brown skin, and has dark freckles on his face. He has on one of those old timer hats, with the crease on the top of it. The man walks slowly, but has no need for a cane. He takes his time making it up the steps, and into Dean's building.

Dean is thinking how to tell Dawn, especially since they are mad at each other. To his relief, Dawn is watching them from her door's peep hole. She comes out of her door and looks at the old man, then at Dean, then back at the old man. She comes close to his face, and stares real hard.

"Papa?" She mumbles out, and then looks at Dean.

"Of all the low down things you could have done." She walks up to him, slaps him in the face, and then enters her apartment. She slams the door behind her, and you hear her screaming in her apartment. You also hear what sounds like glass braking. Dean is unaffected by the slap, as the man looks at him.

"You OK." Papa asks.

"Yeah, I'm fine. You see we were friends when I found your location, and sent you the ticket to come here, but much has changed since." Dean explains.

"Maybe I should have waited until you two are friends again." Papa states. "I'm too old to get slapped."

"No she will be back out for you. Just wait here by her door." Dean states.

Dean walks over to Dawn's door, and yells to her. "He will be out here when you're ready." Dean states.

"You sure this is a good idea?" Papa asks.

"I'm sure." Dean encourages him. "It's all a big shock to her, but she will open the door."

Dean is about to enter his apartment, but Papa speaks to him.

"Man, she has grown so big and so beautiful. It's hard to believe she is that same little girl I used to play with." Papa states.

"She is not." Dean replies.

"I hope she hears me." Papa states a little nervous.

"Talk from your heart, and not your ego." Dean warns.

Papa thinks for a second, and nods his head to him.

"Whatever happens, thanks for finding me, and leading me to her." Papa states.

Dean nods to him, and enters his apartment.

Dawn's ranting has quieted down, as Papa listens to the door. He looks for something to sit on, but sees nothing. He then leans against the wall, looking a little worried. After about fifteen minutes, he hears footsteps from behind the door. He does not know for sure, but feels Dawn is peeking at him through the peep hole. He can feel eyes watching him. He looks towards the peep hole, but then looks away. He feels a little uneasy.

"He has you standing out in the hall." Dawn's voice states from behind the door.

The lock is heard turning, and the door opens slightly. Papa looks at it as his invitation to enter the apartment. Dawn is standing there looking at him. Papa looks tired and looks at the couch.

"Can I sit down" He asks.

Dawn looks at him, and points to the couch. He takes a seat, and Dawn takes a seat at the other end of the couch. She is still staring at him.

"Well aren't you going to say something?" Papa asks.

"I have thought about this moment many nights. Thinking just how I was going to curse you out for leaving me. Even now, I can't believe you are in front of me. I still feel angry, but deep inside. I want to know why you left?" Dawn states.

"I had many vices, which the two popular ones were alcohol and gambling. When I had to choose between the two it was alcohol that won. Your mother knew I shouldn't be around you so she got an order of protection to keep me away from you. She stated I was hurting you, especially because of the refrigerator incident. You remember that?" Papa asks.

"Everyday of my life." Dawn states. "How did Mama find out about that? I didn't tell her. Wait, how did you find out?" Dawn asks.

"A neighbor cursed me out about it, and then finally got around to telling your mother. She went crazy on me, and had me arrested. I could no longer come to the house to see you or visit you at your school. Your mother is a wild woman, but she was right in what she did. I loved you, but I loved my gambling and alcohol more. No one could stop me from watching you from afar. I can still see you walking to school, like a little lady. You would look so cute in your uniform. I always wanted to grab you and hug you, but I knew I could not." Papa states as he wipes the tears from his eyes. Dawn is also crying, but she is looking away from him.

"I said I wasn't going to cry if I saw you again. I didn't come here to cry. I came to say sorry, and to thank you. I'm sorry for being responsible for you being locked in the refrigerator, I'm sorry for being a rotten dad." Papa states as he can no longer hold back the tears. He is looking at Dawn. "I'm sorry for all the broken promises, for all the birthday parties I missed, for all the tears you shed because of me, and the tears you shed that I could not help you wipe. I'm an old, old man now, and I don't know how much longer I got to live. I am glad I had this chance to behold my baby girl once more, and to apologize for the wrong I have done." Papa states, as he opens his arms to her, and she comes running over to him.

They cry in each other arms for a few minutes. Papa then looks at her.

"Baby girl, I have done my part. I have asked for your forgiveness from the bottom of my heart. If you forgive me or not is between you and God. I also wanted to thank you for saving me." Papa states.

Dawn looks at him puzzled while still in his arms.

"You see, after your mother barred me from seeing you, I got locked up for robbery. I did my time, and came out drinking heavier then ever. By then you and your mother had moved away, and no one would tell me where you went. When I hit rock bottom, I met a lady I fell in love with. She helped me get over my alcohol addiction, but it was your face that gave me strength. I thought about you every time I felt like drinking again. It was your face that kept me going. I had your picture by my side the entire time. I never drank again. I got married, had two children, and live in Chicago all these years. I just buried my wife, when I heard from Dean. He hired a private investigator to find me. He used information he got from your mother, during her visit. The investigator found me and here I am. Your half brother and sister are in college now, but I told them all about you. We would even say a prayer for you at night." Papa states.

"I missed you, and I'm glad you have changed your life. I just wished you could have done it for me when I was younger." Dawn says.

"I wish I could have too. I was there for my family. I held a steady job and supported them. My only sadness was wondering what you were going through, and were you safe." Papa states.

"You have me now." Dawn states with a smile.

"Yes I do, and I won't drop the ball this time. You can come visit me as often as you want in Chicago. I also want your half brother and sister to meet you." Papa states.

"I would like that." Dawn answers.

CHAPTER THIRTY TWO:
THE RE-EDUCATION OF JASON

Jason is knocking on Tammy's door.

"Who is it?" The voice asks innocently from behind the door.

"Me." Jason states.

"Let's not do this again." Tammy states.

"I won't start anything this time. Just open the door. so I won't have to say this to the door." Jason asks her.

Tammy opens the door. He steps inside. "Please just answer this question. Have you been with the guy again?" Jason asks calmly, but he is biting his lip literally.

"I never got the chance the first time. I was going to get back at you, but then some dummy turned the power off, and we got tacks in our feet. Afterwards I told him it was a mistake, and I have not seen him since." Tammy states. "How many have you been with? Tell me the truth."

"When I was with you I was with a lot of girls." Jason says, as Tammy's face frowns up.

"But wait. Since we were apart I have had the chance to be with a few ladies, but I did not want them. I was a fool for cheating on you. You treated me so well, and I treated you wrong. Seeing you with that other man gave me a dose of how wrong I have been to you. If you take me back, I promise you things will be different." Jason pleads.

"You have never apologized for anything in your life, but I can't trust you."

"You can hire a private eye to follow me around anytime you want. I'll pay for it, but you can hire him. I promise you from now on. I will be faithful. I love you and I don't want to blow it again." Jason explains.

"I don't know." Tammy says.

"Look. Cupid is Stupid." Jason states.

"What?" Tammy asks with a smile.

"You heard me. Cupid is stupid. Pass on me and you never know what you're going to get. Cupid is stupid, but we don't have to be. Don't pass me up. I know you have every right to, but I am here begging, pleading, and crying." Jason states. Tammy looks in shock.

"Baby, you're crying. You never cry." Tammy looks at him with sympathy.

"I never had a reason, until now." Jason states.

"Hold on." Tammy closes the door, as Jason wonders what is going on.

"Come on in." He hears Tammy say from inside the apartment. Jason enters and shuts the door, but the apartment is dark.

"I'm in the bedroom." Tammy states, as Jason starts smiling to himself. He makes his way to the bedroom. He sees Tammy is on the bed with a night gown on. She has candles lit on the headboard, so he can see her in the dark room. As he gets to the door, Tammy states, "I heard you begging, but you were not on your knees. I want you to come to me on your knees because you're going to have to lick your forgiveness out of me."

Jason gladly gets on his knees, and makes his way towards her vagina. As he gets a few feet in the room, he falls on his back, and yells in pain. Tammy turns on the lights, and Jason has tacks in one of his knees.

"Now we are even." Tammy states, as she turn on the light, and comes over to him. She pulls out the three tacks that are in his right knee. She then lays on him.

"Are you too hurt to do something?" Tammy asks as she kisses his lips.

"I'm fine." Jason states as he kisses her back. He then stops. "I love you, and am satisfied with just holding you again."

"Look at you. You're so sweet now, but I need the lust part right now. Baby it has been a while." Tammy states as she starts kissing him on his neck.

CHAPTER THIRTY THREE: THE RE-EDUCATION OF JENNIFER

Daren is making a phone call from a pay phone, and his car is parked in front of a strip bar.

"Baby don't hang up. Listen to me. I feel I'm loosing you, and I don't want our marriage to continue on like this. I was about to enter a strip bar for the first time in our marriage. I suddenly came to my senses and realized my wife has the perfect body.

When I married you six years ago, I did not marry you just to have children. Baby hear this. I love you, and I want you. I don't care about children.

"Then why do you want to have sex all the time?" Jennifer asks him over the phone. It is obvious in her voice that she is crying.

"Because every time I look at you I go crazy. I want you, and there is nothing wrong with that. I can live life without children, but I can't live life without you. Now let me know can you live life without children?" Daren asks. "I am not ready for this marriage to end over some bullshit."

"But I can't even give you a seed. I don't feel like a complete woman." Jennifer complains.

"Look. You care for me, work, and do a lot around the home. How dare you say you're not a complete women. You are perfect. A woman is not defined by how many children she has. A complete woman to me is someone who takes care of their man, and lets no one come between them. All you have to do to make me happy, is put it dawn, every time it goes up, and love me. Can you do that?" Daren asks.

"I can do that baby. So you're ok without children?" Jennifer asks.

"I'm fine without it."

"You have to do me a favor. Be home in ten minutes, or I'm going to start with out you. Hello-hello—." Jennifer states, but then hears the dial tone. Daren is in his car speeding home, as he left the phone off the hook.

"I'm twenty minutes away." He states, as he speeds up.

Daren is zooming through traffic. He speeds by a yellow light, and a police officer follows him with his siren on. The police car is telling him to pull over, but Daren is not listening.

Daren looks back, and then at his watch. A cloud appears over his head. It is Jennifer in a night gown, looking at her watch.

"Oh hell no." Daren thinks to himself, as he speeds up.

"He is not stopping. I repeat he is not stopping. Send back up. I am heading south on Main street." The officer states over the radio.

Jennifer gets into bed. She is waiting and smiling. She hears all these sirens, and sees the cop lights in her window. She looks out her window, and sees five cop cars in front of her house, and Daren's car. Daren shows up at the bedroom door.

"Honey what are all these cop cars doing here?" Jennifer asks.

"I didn't notice. Let's do this." Daren states.

Outside the house the bedroom light goes off. The police come out, and pull their guns out.

"Come out peacefully, and with your hands up." An officer is heard saying.

"Give me fifteen minutes. I'll be right out." Daren yells from the house, as the officers look around puzzled.

Twenty minutes later, Daren comes out with a smile on his face. He is arrested, as some of the neighbors watch.

"Officer, you don't understand. I had to rush to my wife. She was sick, and I was sick, but we are better now. I had to get home quick." Daren tries to explain.

Gary walks in among the officers, and Jennifer comes running out the house.

"Officers I told him there was an emergency home, so he came rushing home. It was my fault." Jennifer states.

"That may be true, but we have to sort this out down town." An officer tells Jennifer, as he puts Daren into a police car.

"Leave that man alone. He is not a criminal; he is a Social worker. He was just trying to get home to his wife." Gary states.

"Sir you have to leave the area." An officer tells him.

"Don't you sir me." Gary states, and the officer grabs his night stick. Oh you are going to use your night stick. Use your night stick. Go ahead hurt me." Gary says loudly, as the officer stands there looking at him. Gary turns his back slightly, and pokes out his buttocks. "Come on use that big old night stick. They only call it a night stick because you like to beat Black people with it." A captain a few feet away hears Gary's voice, and he acts like he is hearing something familiar.

"No, I'm not going to use my night stick." An officer states to Gary.

"Well how about the other things, what you got?" Gary asks.

207

The officer starts moving Gary back.

"Stop pushing me. I want to see the captain." Gary states.

"I want to see the Captain also." Jennifer says, as she stands there with Gary.

"Captain, can you deal with this please." The officer says, as the Captain walks over.

"Ok. What's the problem?" The Captain asks. The Captain sees Gary and blushes. Gary looks at him.

"Boolishus?" Gary asks.

"Hi, can we keep it down?" The Captain asks, as he pulls Gary to the side.

"Hi, I didn't recognize you without the wig. I didn't know you are a real cop. I should have known though, because you pretended so well."

"Look I need to keep this quiet." The Captain states.

"Hey, I know the rules. What happened at the Pink Flamingo stays at the Pink Flamingo." Gary states.

"That is right. Look, is your friend trying to break the law or what?" The Captain asks.

"No. He was having marriage problems, and wanted to get home to his wife. That is all." Gary explains.

"OK. I'm going to let him go, but I'll cuff you later." The Captain states.

"No. I'm sorry I can't deal with people who are scared to come out the closet." Gary states, and then walks away, but then comes back. "Unless we do it in a closet."

CHAPTER THIRTY FOUR:
A FRIEND TO THE END

Dean is sleeping in his bed, and there is a knock on his door. Dean wakes up and walks slowly to the door.

"Who is it?" Dean asks.

"It's me." Dawn states.

"What do you want at this time?" Dean asks without opening the door.

"I need your help. It's important." Dawn states, as Dean opens the door to see a very tired Dawn.

"Ask Barry." Dean states as he starts to walk away from the door.

"He can't help me. I told you we broke up. He says I was too into you, and so he got into someone else. I'm not hurt over it though, just disappointed" Dawn states.

"I still can't help you." Dean tells her as he is about to close the door.

"Thanks for bringing my father here to see me. We did some soul mending. Seeing him settled a lot of demons I had inside of me. I'm going to visit him Christmas, and he wants you to come." Dawn states.

"I know. He stopped by before he left." Dean states as he is about to close the door again.

"You said you loved me once. If you have a shred of love for me still, please let me in." Dawn states. "You see I'm in that elevator again. I have been there for a few days, and can't get out. I thought by seeing my father I would be fine, but I am still there."

Dean opens the door, and she is tearing a little.

"I have a big presentation tomorrow. I know you hate me, and don't want me here, but I have not slept right in four days. I have tried everything. Please I have to sleep or I will not make it through tomorrow. I won't ask you to do this ever again. I promise." Dawn begs.

Dean walks into the apartment, as Dawn closes the door and follows. They both walk in to the bedroom. Dean opens up the covers and lies down. Dawn goes over to the CD. player and puts in a disk.

"I just want you to hear something. I just want to answer a question you asked me. You asked how you feel to me. This song describes it best." Dawn states.

The song, "More than words," by Extreme is playing. Dawn lies down on Dean. She looks at his face, and deep into his eyes, as the song plays. Dawn talks to him.

"My Father was my entire life, but he constantly broke his promise to me. It scarred me for life, but those wounds are healing now. All my life I have been looking for someone who could take his place. I created an imaginary friend to help me cope. I couldn't keep believing in an imaginary friend, so I looked to other men, but there was no one. I thought there was someone, but he turned out to be un-trust worthy. That is the person I lost my virginity to. You were there for me, in a way that I wanted you to be there for me. My guiding light leading me out of the refrigerator. You continued to be there for me. When I saw you with my friend, it hurt because you are mine in a sense. I know I have no claim on you and it is selfish, but you're what I have been searching for all my life, but not sexually." Dawn explains.

"Cheryl is cool and all, but that was a booty call. Nothing more. I knew I should not have, but it was there, and I was getting tired of waiting for you. I know now that love should never grow tired of waiting." Dean states.

"It's not your fault because my insides are all messed up. It's getting better since I met my father." Dawn answers.

"You feel hurt because you caught me once. Think about all the times you went out with Barry, and how I felt. Then you would come home, and talk about how you went dancing, or out to eat." Dean states.

"I now see how that made you feel, but it was not my intention to hurt you. I'll say this one thing and then go to sleep. I need your friendship. I need you here. That is the most important thing in the world to me. Now that is love, just not sexual love." Dawn states.

"I can't. It hurts to be with you, and not have you. It hurts a little less to not be with you, and not have you." Dean explains.

"I understand." Dawn states. "And even with Barry gone, I still don't feel you like that."

"What happened with Barry?"

"He tried to make me choose between you and him. Guess who I chose." Dawn states.

"Let's get some sleep." Dean states.

"OK."

Dawn lies on Dean, and seems to fall fast asleep. Dean lies in bed staring up at the ceiling, listening to the song. "Rejection stings." He thinks.

CHAPTER THIRTY FIVE:
LOVE SICK? OR IS LOVE SICK

It is the next day, and Dean is watching TV. when the phone rings.

"Hello.---Where are you? What about your mother? Cheryl? None of them are around. ---OK. But you better be near death."

Dean grabs some medication, and goes to Dawn's apartment. He opens the door, and goes to Dawn's room. He covers his nose, as he sees her lying in bed sick. She has vomit on the bed, floor, and her clothing. Dawn looks at him, and faintly whispers.

"Help me. I feel like I am dying. I have to use the bathroom, but I am too weak to stand on my own." Dawn states.

"You need an ambulance." Dean states as he walks over to her.

"No hospitals. I just need your help." Dawn pleads.

Dean runs over to her, and she leans on him to get out of bed. He walks her to the bathroom, and pulls off all her clothes. He sits her on the toilet, and runs out the bathroom to get air. He then goes back in with his shirt over his nose. He feels her head and gets the thermometer to take her temperature. He puts the thermometer in her mouth, and runs bath water. He takes her clothing and her dirty sheets, and puts it in a black garbage bag. He comes back and checks her temperature.

"You have a fever." Dean states.

"I feel like I need to throw up." Dawn says.

Dean runs and gets a mop bucket. Dawn throws up into the bucket. Dean gets a piece of tissue, and wipes her face. He then starts rubbing her back trying to soothe her. Dawn wipes herself, as Dean waits until she is finished. He does not want to see her wipe herself, but has to stay close in case she falls. Dean then helps Dawn into the bathtub. She gets in slowly, as Dean helps her ease down in the water.

"This will not help your fever, but you need a bath." Dean states, as he also hands her a drink. "This is ginger ale with real ginger in it. It should help your stomach settle."

Dawn sips it slowly, as she looks at Dean. "I am too weak to wash up. You have to help me."

Dean takes the wash cloth and starts washing her body. He starts with her face, as Dawn is sitting there with her eyes closed, still sipping the drink. He then works his way down to her nice breasts, but he is nowhere near thinking anything sexual. Dawn has briefly gone topless in front of Dean. When she was changing her clothes and talking to him, or just coming out of the shower, Dean may catch a quick glimpse. She really thought of him like a girlfriend, and did not try to hide her body from him: however, she did not try to flaunt it either. She would have never gotten completely naked in front of him.

This time is different because Dawn is sick, and was a little more negotiable. There is still a part of Dawn that is mind-full of his hands, and how long they stay in a certain area. She is making sure he does not try to cop a feel. If he did, then that will definitely put a damper on their friendship. He could wash her breast, but grabbing it is a feel. She knows that Dean is not that type of person, and would actually be shock if he tried to cop a feel.

Besides, she smelled like vomit, and wanted to get that smell off of her. She is sure he's not enjoying this, because of the look of disgust on his face. He looks like he could throw up any minute, but the smell is starting to go away. All in all Dean still looks at her like she is Queen; even if she is a sick Queen.

Dean starts washing her legs, arms, and face.

"I need my private areas washed. I trust you." Dawn states as Dean turns to her. Dawn spread her legs in the tub. He vagina could not be seen, but he is about to rub it. It is nothing sensual about it Dean thought. He is only touching it via a wash cloth. He still had the smell of her throw up in her mind, so he is not thinking anything sexual; however, when he looked at her sick and all, he still has to admire how beautiful she still looks. Dean washes her private areas. Dawn even lifts up a little so Dean could wash her butt.. Den then let her soak, while he makes her bed.

Dean returns to the bathroom, with Dawn's pajamas and a towel. He takes the towel, and helps her up. He wraps the towel around her.

"Now it's cold." Dawn states.

Dean lifts her to the bed, and dries her off.

"It should feel good in here. I put the oven on, just until you get into bed." Dean states, as he continues to dry all over her body. He then starts to put her underwear on.

"I need my lotion please. My skin gets dry without it.

"But you're sick."

"That is still no reason to be ashy." Dawn states as she hands him the lotion.

Dean rubs the lotion all over her body. Dawn is shivering.

"You're still cold?" Dean asks.

A little, but I will be fine." Dawn answers.

He is rubbing lotion on her breasts, and it is turning him on, but he ignores his impulses. It's hard not to be turned on since she does not have an odor anymore. Dean sees her nipples get real hard, and she has these dark, large round nipples. It is driving Dean crazy, but he would not violate her trust by making sure she has the most lotion breasts in NYC. Even as he ran his hands over her plump butt, he did not give it any extra time. He is amazed at how she is letting him do these things. He then puts lotion on her inner thighs right next to her vagina. He does not look at it because he can see Dawn looking at him. Once again the throw up smell is still fresh in his mind, and it would also be extremely tacky to try something.

He then puts on her underwear and Pajamas, but his dick so hard, that it is starting to hurt. He helps her under the covers.

"You're staying here right? Don't leave me." Dawn asks

"Yes, I am staying." Dean states as he gives her some medicine.

"What is this for?" Dawn asks.

"To help your stomach. I just think you have a stomach virus. Are you hungry?' Dean asks.

"No."

"OK. Try to get some rest."

Dawn looks at him with the most sincere smile. Like how a baby smiles at a parent or a person being rescued smiles at the person who saved them.

"I want my kiss before I go to sleep." Dawn states.

"No way. You have vomit breath." Dean states and laughs. Dawn laughs too.

"You wouldn't kiss me with vomit breath. I would kiss you." Dawn states.

Dean walks over to her and pecks her on the lips. Dawn pushes him away as soon as their lips touch.

"You're right. Please get my tooth brush, and some toothpaste." Dawn asks him.

Dean goes to the bathroom, and comes back with a toothbrush with toothpaste on it. Dean starts brushing her teeth, as Dawn loves the attention. He then goes to the bathroom, and comes back with some water. Dawn rinses her mouth, and spits it out in the empty throw up bucket, which is by the bed.

Dawn smiles at him again, and closes her eyes, as Dean sits in the chair by her bed. Dawn re-opens them. She motions to Dean to come lay down with her. Dean takes off his shoes, and lies on the bed. She lies on his chest. She falls fast asleep. Later in the night, Dean is uncomfortable with Dawn sleeping on him. He gets up, very carefully as not to wake her. He then sleeps in the reclining chair, by the bed. Dawn wakes up, sees him in the chair, and joins him. She takes a blanket to cover them.

Later that night, Dean wakes up with her crowding him in the chair. He then goes to the bed to sleep. Dawn wakes up because of his movements, and joins him on the bed. She cuddles close to him.

It is morning, and Dean is waking up. He turns and sees Dawn staring at him.

"We slept about fourteen hours. I feel much better, and I am hungry. That is a good sign right?" Dawn asks.

"Yeah, I'll get you some toast and tea." Dean states.

"I feel like bacon." Dawn states.

"No grease or dairy, or you will get sick again." Dean warns.

Dean gets up and puts some water in the kettle.

They eat breakfast and then Dean lies across the bed. He is still a little tired or traumatized by yesterday's events. Too tired to notice the strange quietness that has settled on Dawn. Maybe he figured she is embarrassed he has seen her naked. He doesn't notice the strange way she is looking at him. Like he had something that belongs to her, and she wants it back. He still seems tired. Dawn comes out of the bathroom.

"My teeth are all clean. No more throw up breath. I feel like I have my strength back. Thank you doctor." Dawn states.

"Good. You can wash the dishes." Dean jokes.

Dawn comes over to him, and lies on top of him.

"What you did for me, there are no words to express." She states as her eyes start to water. "You showed me something last night. When I was at my worse, you were there for me."

"I did what any good friend would do." Dean states.

"What you did went beyond words. That was what the song I let you listen to is about. Your love is action, and I was right about choosing you." Dawn states.

"Right about what?" Dean asks.

"Remember Barry wanted me to choose between you and him. He said that I am obsessed with you because I'm always talking about you. He also did not like the way I laid on you, and kissed you on the lips." Dawn states.

"If only he could see us now." Dean states jokingly. He can not believe she is lying on top of him. She has never done that before, but he is not mad at her. He just keeps waiting to hear the part that he knows is coming. The we can only be friend's part.

"It doesn't matter if Barry sees us. I broke up with him."

"So you gave up the football star, and all his fame and money?" Dean asks.

"All superficial. Isn't it love, when you don't want to lose something, you're willing to let all other things go?" Dawn asks.

"Love is too vast to define."

"Don't make it mystical. It is right here in our faces." Dawn states.

"Ah Cupid is stupid as your mother says." Dean answers.

"Naw, Cupid is not stupid, we are."

"What are you saying?"

"I just want to try something, but I may stop suddenly. Just bear with me for a second." Dawn states as she looks into his eyes. She also hops off of him, and lies besides him. She lays there for a few seconds, as Dean looks at her. Dawn takes his hand and rubs it against her stomach. She then holds it up and looks at it like she is trying to decide something. She then runs his hand from her upper stomach to under her panties.

Dean could not believe that his hand kept getting lower and lower, until he felt the wetness of her vagina. He looks at Dawn's face, and she is turned on by it. He starts to kiss her, as he gently rubs her click. Dawn's body starts to shiver, as Dean can not believe this is real. He believes he is dreaming. Dawn closes her eyes and starts moaning, as they are tongue kissing. He starts feeling her buttocks, and her groans become more intense. He can feel her wet pussy moving against his arm, as he is rubbing her fat butt. She pulls down his pants, takes off her pajama pants, and her underwear. She starts rubbing her vagina against his penis. Dawn is on top, with her eyes closed, and her breathing becomes more erotic.

She opens her eyes to see him looking into her face. She reaches down and starts kissing his lips, and then raises back up to get more feeling. Dean is rubbing her breasts, as he can not believe he is about to make love with Dawn, the lady of his dreams. She had these big dark nipples. The sight of them makes Dean's dick get harder, as if that was possible. His dick feels like the incredible hulk, and Dawn is making him angry, but she is gonna like him more when he gets angry.

Dawn's moans gets loud as she closes her eyes again. She stops for a quick second, and pulls a condom out of nowhere. She puts it on him fast, and then uses her body to maneuver the penis into her vagina.

"Oh shit." Dawn whispers to herself, as her eyes close tight again.

Dean feels that tight pussy and thinks Barry must have a small dick because he did nothing to loosen up Dawn's tight pussy. He then wonders why is he thinking about Barry's dick, and continues to focus on the pussy at hand. He likes a tight pussy, but he doesn't want to cum too fast, yet he doesn't want to slow Dawn down. He looks at her face and could tell she is ready to release. He knows he is about to as well. He grabs her butt, and starts bouncing her up in the air. She starts screaming louder, and doesn't seem to care who hears her. Her eyes look like they are rolled up in the back of her head, as she jumps off of him.

"Leave" She states, as he busts his nut into a condom. He looks at her puzzled, and she won't even look at him. "Just leave please."

"That is just plain rude. I could have missed my nut." Dean thinks, but he gets up, and puts on his pants. He picks up his shoes, and leaves the apartment. He does not know what is going on. He retraces his steps and found nothing he did wrong. He thought she was about to cum. He though that maybe she asked him to leave because she was not feeling him sexually. She just wanted to give him a little something. Or maybe she saw that he had cum, and was mad because she didn't get hers. Whatever the problem, he is left alone and confused in his own apartment. He goes to take a shower.

CHAPTER THIRTY SIX:
THE RE-EDUCATION OF DAWN

Dawn lies in her bed, her body still shaking. Her body had gone into convulsions, but Dean did not notice it because he was busting his nut. Dawn is still sweating, as she gets up, and makes a phone call.

A half an hour later, Dawn is dressed and talking with Cheryl in her living room.

"I wanted to call my mother, but I can't talk to her about this. Thanks for coming over." Dawn states.

"So how did this all come about." Cheryl asks.

"He did something to me. I think he cast a spell on me or something. I was sick yesterday, and he gave me a bath. He was putting lotion on my butt, and it just all of a sudden felt good. I was sick, but my body started shivering at his touch. It's like he was rubbing electricity on me. I have never felt nothing like it.

"Ah huh, so then what?" Cheryl asks.

"In the morning, I want to see if this was real. I put his hand on my vagina, and my body went crazy. The bedroom was shaking girl." Dawn states with a serious look on her face.

"What do you mean? Oh he did that move where he---" Cheryl starts to say, but Dawn cuts her off.

"No. Well he did that, but something in me shook like the Earth was shaking. My entire body was jerking, and I couldn't control it. All my energy just left me. All my hurt and all my pain just released."

"Wait, you never got your big one before?" Cheryl asks.

"Big one? Big What? Oh you mean those orgasms." Dawn asks puzzled.

"Not those little orgasms. It's the big one." Cheryl explains.

Dawn thinks for a while, and states, "That is what it was. It was so intense it scared the hell out of me."

"Yeah girl, where you been?" Cheryl asks jokingly.

"That was my first one." Dawn states shyly.

"Well it sounds like you had a good one." Cheryl states.

Dawn looks at her seriously, and starts to tear.

"It scared me. I didn't know what was going on. My feelings for him are off the charts now." Dawn states.

"I was hoping to have him, but he was never mine. When did you start feeling for him?" Cheryl asks.

"I guess when I saw how he was caring for me, and how he was there for me. He washed me up, rubbed me down with lotion, and it felt so good. He was caring for me even though he was mad at me. While he was rubbing lotion on me, my feeling grew so intense. He didn't even try to get a cheap feel, and I thought to myself. This man really loves me. I don't want to hear him say it. I want to see him say it, and feel him say it."

Dawn pauses for a few seconds.

"So I am not crazy. The Earth didn't shake, it was me right? I mean everything is normal, and he did not put a spell on me?" Dawn asks.

"Everything is far from normal, you are crazy, the Earth did quake, and he did cast a spell on you." Cheryl states as he looks at her smiling. "You're in love, and you realize that now."

"I can be selfish at times, but I swear I would take a bullet for him." Dawn states with a serious look on her face.

"That is how you feel right now. That is a part of love." Cheryl states.

"You just lost me right then." Dawn tells her.

"Well. There will be times you will want to take a bullet for him, and then there will be times when you will want to put a bullet in him. It's all love."

They both laugh.

"Cupid is stupid." Dawn states.

"The stupidest guy of all." Cheryl says, but them smiles at Dawn. "But you're not."

"No, not any more." Dawn states.

"Love will always be tested, but true love will survive the test and hardships." Cheryl says.

"It's like these feeling were deep inside of me all along, but now they are out on the surface. I got to go see him, but I have to do something first." Dawn states.

Cheryl looks at her, as she leaves.

CHAPTER THIRTY SEVEN: CUPID'S REVENGE

It has been five hours since Dean left Dawn's apartment, and he still has not heard from her. Dean is on the couch thinking, and there is a knock at the door.

"Come in." Dean states, as Dawn walks in. Dean is looking at her. She is staring at him. She walks in slowly, and sits beside him.

"How are you?" Dean asks.

"I have never been better. It all makes sense now because I understand everything perfectly." Dawn states.

"Well can you explain it to me because I can't understand why I had to leave earlier?" Dean states.

Dawn is looking at him with amazement. "I could hardly walk when I entered and saw you. You make my knees buckle. What happened this morning was a manifestation of what was happening all along. I knew it, but was too scared of it." Dawn says.

"What were you scared of?" Dean asks.

"Of you, and of true love. That is why I kept you close and in my arms, but at a true love distance. I did all this involuntarily. Kissing you, but never kissing you. Holding you, but never touching you. Yesterday, you showed me that you are truly dedicated to me. Any man that will see me like that, and still love me, is real." Dawn says.

"I've been saying that all along."

"Remember with me, it's more than words. Remember the song? That is love to me. You showed me what all the words in the world couldn't say." Dawn states. She pauses for a few seconds, and then continues.

"I was traumatized by the relationship I had with my father. He was never there for me, and so I felt that there was no man that will ever be there for me." Dawn states, as she gets up, and is messing with the CD. Player.

"So are you and Cheryl done for good?" Dawn asks.

"You know we are." Dean answers.

"Just one more question." Dawn comes over to him, and gets on her knees as she lies in his lap.

"What?" Dean asks.

"Your place, mine, or a new place." Dawn asks.

"What do you mean new?" Dean asks puzzled.

"The furniture? Will we live here or at my place or find a new place because I will never sleep another night without you." Dawn asks, as she pulls something out of her pocket. She looks up into his face.

"Will you marry me?" Dawn asks.

Dean is floored. He can't believe it. Dawn has a ring, and is asking him to marry her. He never thought he would be getting engaged, when he woke up next to her this morning.

The CD. player starts playing "Step in the name of Love," by R. Kelly.

"Yes I'll marry you." Dawn gets up, and Dean gets up as they start hugging. Then they start kissing, and then dancing.

CHAPTER THIRTY EIGHT: THIS WEEK'S STATISTICS. CUPID: WINS - 6 : LOSES - 37,482

Six month later, three couples are getting married by a preacher. R. Kelly's song is still playing, as Dean and Dawn, Jason and Tammy, Tonka and Carmen are getting married, while Daren and Jennifer watch. Dean is giving his vows to Dawn.

"Many people today do not know what love is, but I'm going to tell you the creator's definition of love, which is given in 1 Corinthians 13:4. You know why, because that is the way I feel about you." He says to Dawn.

"Love is patient and kind, never jealous or envious, never boastful or proud, and never haughty or selfish or rude. Love does not demand its own way. It is not irritable or touchy. It does not hold grudges and will hardly even notice when others do it wrong. It is never glad about injustice, but rejoices whenever truth wins out. If you love someone, you will be loyal to him/her no matter what the cost. You will always believe in them, always expect the best of them, and always stand your ground in defending them."

Dean looks deeper into her eyes.

"When I was a child, I loved as a child; now that I am a man, I love as a man should, and has put away childish things. I will always love you as a man should."

They kiss each other.

The three married couples are later shown dancing on the dance floor, and Daren and Jennifer come and join them. Jennifer is a little fatter then she was before.

"You sure you want to dance. I don't want to strain the baby." Dean states.

"I'm only three months silly." Jennifer answers.

"All my friends are married. It's something. Cupid is Stupid. No one would have thought we all would all have been married, seven months ago." Daren states as he looks at his friends dancing.

"Maybe Cupid is not so stupid after all." Jennifer states.

All four couples are seen dancing on the dance floor.

Author Biography

Aaron Bryant was born and raised in Queens, NY. He read poetry in grade school, but started writing poetry in high school. He also started writing stories for his friends in class to read. In high school, Aaron Bryant won a few poetry/writing contests. One of which was a City wide contest. There was a teacher who tough Aaron's poetry to her class. In his college years, he taught himself to write screenplays, and presently has six screenplays. One of which is Cupid is Stupid, which he decided to make his first professional book.

To April,

Thanks for your help. I hope you enjoy the book.